MW00624854

Photo by Madeleine Donovan

Thom Donovan is a classically trained musician and published songwriter who has spent his career recording and touring worldwide in rock bands. *The Twin Affair* is his debut novel. He lives in Nashville with his wife and son.

THE TWIN AFFAIR

Thom Donovan

THE TWIN AFFAIR

Vanguard Press

VANGUARD PAPERBACK

© Copyright 2023
Thom Donovan

The right of Thom Donovan to be identified as author of
this work has been asserted by him in accordance with the
Copyright, Designs and Patents Act 1988.

All Rights Reserved

No reproduction, copy or transmission of this publication
may be made without written permission.
No paragraph of this publication may be reproduced,
copied or transmitted save with the written permission of the
publisher, or in accordance with the provisions
of the Copyright Act 1956 (as amended).

Any person who commits any unauthorised act in relation to
this publication may be liable to criminal
prosecution and civil claims for damages.

A CIP catalogue record for this title is
available from the British Library.

ISBN 978 1 80016 617 2

Vanguard Press is an imprint of
Pegasus Elliot Mackenzie Publishers Ltd.
www.pegasuspublishers.com

This is a work of fiction. Names, characters, businesses, places,
events, and incidents are either the product of the author's
imagination or used in a fictitious manner. Any resemblance to
actual persons, living or dead, or actual events is purely
coincidental.

First Published in 2023

Vanguard Press
Sheraton House Castle Park
Cambridge England

Printed & Bound in Great Britain

To Madeleine and Julian

Acknowledgements

This book would not exist without the support and wisdom of my wife, Madeleine. I am equally grateful to my son, Julian, for his endless curiosity and light.

Thanks to my family, especially my father—a great storyteller in the Irish tradition.

Music provided a path for me to see the world; I couldn't have written this story without it. The people and places I've visited changed my life.

We tell stories to understand the human condition. What motivates us? What corrupts us? What, if anything, can save us? *The Twin Affair* is a story about identity—who we are now versus the people we used to be. This book is my attempt at something like understanding these things.

And yet all this might have been endured,
if not approved, by the mad revelers around.

The Masque of the Red Death
— Edgar Allan Poe

1

Morning, Mr Gadly

A t the threshold, she wondered if this job would change her life.

The morning ritual began this way. Maggie dropped the keys, reaching to gather yesterday's mail-shot through the letterbox. She separated the mail between personal and business and arranged the latter on the staircase railing for Caitlin, the accountant, to collect. Maggie's office is on the second floor. The old building, like a brownstone you might find in Brooklyn, sits on a lazy street in midtown Nashville.

With the shades open, the sun put light on the drab old interior. A sophisticated exterior created an illusion to what lived inside—dowdy furniture and paint. The smell of freshly brewed coffee changed the routine into something tolerable.

A temporary reprieve because it's on to collecting dishes dirtied and abandoned by her colleagues. Her co-worker's education places them above the burden of having to clean up after themselves. A perverse job, cleaning an adult mess. The filth of an adult is much worse than what's left behind by children. Children have a good excuse for being messy brutes—they don't know better. The adult, by definition, has developed past the rearing stage—though even a casual observance of sapiens dismisses this myth with ease. The scene is a lab experiment where coffee cups become petri dishes and discarded lattes set off into bio-agents.

She climbs and descends the stairs in a shift dress and heels, dropping mail onto the intended desks, after having dealt with the above-mentioned culture plates. On her way back up the stairs, she heaves a box of copy paper that was ignored by chivalrous colleagues, carrying it to the storage closet just outside her office. Finally, she pours a cup of coffee, not stale or hot, wipes a dot of sweat from her brow and sits down at her desk to log on for the day.

The desk's minimalist architecture is littered with multi-colored Post-it notes, like sad Christmas lights. Pausing for a breath, the mercy is short-lived as emails flood her inbox with a deluge of both critical and trivial matters. A good deal of time spent sorting through digital epistles laced with spam, deleting and unsubscribing, responding, and forwarding. The forwarded emails will return to her like a boomerang, but it does buy time for dealing with the important things.

The room she occupies is ten feet by twelve feet, or maybe it's twelve feet by fifteen feet. It's quartered with large windows overlooking a quiet street lined with cherry trees. She shares the space with Dan Benchman, an account manager and professional ladder-climber from Chicago. More on him later.

She's the first to arrive, the last to leave, and for the most part, likes her job. Maggie is punctual and reliable. A worker bee inside the office hive. Rules are made to be followed.

The office is home to a public relations and advisory firm called Gadly Group—founded by Richard Gadly, a handsome and erudite lawyer who, before law school, was an aide to the governor. In plain speak, a gofer. It was during those years that Gadly made powerful connections to build his future business. A mix of public affairs and public relations. Policy and commerce—or what difference does it make. Shaping opinions on laws and people. It was about people, he said. Even when it was about the money, it was about the people. Gadly repeated these things until redundancy made them true. As Nashville evolved from a smallish town to a budding metropolis, the recent *it-city* attracted influential people. Gadly looked on with great pride at the expanding skyline. He watched as tower cranes, like modern dinosaurs, moved among the impressive buildings. He did both the moving and the shaking (to use the lingo)—or so he convinced himself.

Gadly enjoyed the lifestyle. He didn't earn enough money for a private jet, but his clients were generous, and he always had a seat on theirs. After years of success, his luck faded. Some clients left when Gadly traded his work for play, so he had to pitch his services to less impressive patrons. Political candidates and CEOs left the spots now occupied by chain restaurants—a depressing reality for Gadly, a man of taste. Gone were the days of schmoozing with tech startups and pro sports expansion teams.

Gadly now stresses over menu items at Murphy's—a chain of Irish pubs created by a man who's never been to Ireland. Everything inside the copied and pasted mess halls is an illusion. The wood is not real wood. The brass is covered in faux patina, and they serve Pepsi instead of Coke. The music is Scottish because the owner doesn't realize that Scotland and Ireland are two different things. The fake Irish pub serves Guinness in a can and pours watered-down domestic beer into glasses made of plastic. It's the kind of place where, if it's your birthday, the staff responds with a ghastly band of tone-deaf workers, trapped in the weeds, pausing to sing to the family, forfeiting tips and falling behind on their tables. If data were to appear showing increased suicide rates from employees, no one would be shocked. Anyone with a soul would dream of the gallows when faced with a lifetime of this humiliating song and dance. The triteness of the organization dangles like a badge of honor. It's what keeps the food pews full.

Returning to our story, Gadly entered the office late in the morning. As always, he was preoccupied and anxious.

"Maggie," Gadly said. He already sounded defeated. "Where is the food reviewer press release for Murphy's?"

"You should have the link now," she said. Resent so the item now rested atop Gadly's inbox.

"Thank you," he said. Down the hall.

"Mr Gadly."

"Yes Maggie?"

"Good morning."

"A good morning it is," he said. The distracted tone faded as he closed his office door.

Little fires. Maggie occupied her day by suppressing small embers of chaos generated by anything to do with public relations. She navigated these hellholes using the language of a cult. She must consider the company's… *tone*. Stay *on message*. Being 'on-brand' is a bizarre catechism of corporate truths. Words are researched and manipulated to influence public behavior. From an ad to a tweet, every publicly released statement has been pored over and spit-shined to convince the public to spend money they don't have on things they don't need. It's psychological warfare.

The burger is awful, and you'll overpay for it, ignoring your family because you're watching sports across eight mind-numbing TV screens, listening to Scottish music in an Irish pub on American soil.

Sorry we don't have Coke. Is Pepsi okay?

Part of Maggie's job is combing social media for customer complaints about the food and building daily reports for Gadly to present to the client. A CODE RED item for Gadly is a family in Akron who'd gotten sick with food poisoning after a night out at Murphy's. Maggie must cajole the sickened family into deleting negative social media posts in exchange for coupons. She obeyed him to the word.

Gadly used to fly first class, now he's stuck in coach. He was depressed about it, but overdue bills won't pay themselves. His fortunes, however, would soon change.

It's crucial to acknowledge, in passing, that Gadly considers himself above second-tier work. Though his business has floundered, he continues to live among high society. He's still invited to parties and is well-liked within upper circles. Over the years he became skilled at convincing others that he was rich regardless of his bank statements. Gadly presented a high-definition version of himself to the world, and he inflated his work like a pufferfish. Maggie was an asset to him, providing the missing warmth to his chilly personality—masking his raw ambition. Now he was in a desperate situation. The debts were mounting, and Gadly needed a fix.

Through her work at the firm, Maggie befriended the office managers who would commiserate on the banalities of the job. Over drinks, a boozy therapy session went something like this:

"My boss has an Ivy League education but still

struggles with a computer," says one assistant to the other.

"Does he do that thing where no matter how many times you tell him, he still overwrites files in the cloud?"

"Oh my God, yes. And then turns into a maniac because he can't find the thing he's just deleted."

Each admonishment is dehumanizing, but they take it because they are professionals. Maggie sometimes feels trapped like a mouse, looking from her window down onto the street. Below she studies people walking dogs or pushing strollers under the heavy leaves of trees. Outside, the sun is warm and inviting, but as it penetrates her window, it's blinding and obtrusive. The tedium of her work makes her feel an absence. She clings to the elusive hope of a promotion and dreams of the day she'll trade running errands for something intellectually worthwhile. But the office is a caste system where assistants are treated like human punching bags. The assistant is a relief valve for executives to release the pressure of stress and insecurity. The ambitious climber is aware there is always someone richer and more talented. This frustrating reality is taken out on the poor sap at the office who doesn't come from a family with the means for a name school and high society.

At office meetings, she sometimes finds the courage to voice suggestions. Gadly adopts her recommendations, but the credit doesn't follow. The idea is plagiarized and repackaged as the original thought of an executive-level employee. And like the mouse, she must attempt the sordid maze all over again.

Maggie didn't seek this life. Growing up in New Orleans, she dreamed of being a comedian. Comedy was her escape hatch from a bitter father and bipolar mother. Her dad was drunk on cheap beer and turned his rage on Maggie and her younger sister, whom she'd protect by absorbing his anger.

The family moved north to a Kansas City suburb when Maggie was in middle school, taking her away from all she knew and loved. She missed her friends, and she missed her grandmother—a sweet, round woman who provided the nurturing component her parents lacked.

In Kansas City, she tried to assimilate with classmates who made fun of her southern accent. She made friends with a Black boy named Lewis, who had just changed schools. They felt like aliens but comforted each other, attending football games, and finding solidarity in an otherwise loud and lonely cafeteria. They hung out in Maggie's bedroom listening to music or watching TV.

One afternoon, Lewis was riding his bicycle to Maggie's house and on the way, he stopped to buy two cans of Dr Pepper—her favorite drink. As he left the parking lot, a car lost control and smashed into him. He died on the spot. Maggie was crushed. She stayed in her house for weeks, missing school, and wondering if her life was destined to repeat this cycle of loss. The natural order of old age was hard but expected. The death of a kid is the touch of Mother Earth's not-so-motherly hand. Life's cards were rigged, she thought.

Her mother wasn't much help either. Maggie never knew which version of Mom would show up. She was despondent and often passed out on the couch. On other days, her mother would vacillate between unhinged madness or crying inconsolably. With Maggie, every insecurity was confirmed. Her parents were too selfish, too drunk, and too damaged to see their cruelty. So, Maggie found solace in books, music, and comedy.

Maggie eventually made friends, and the tomboy grew into a striking young woman with old Hollywood's glamour. She moved out a week after graduation, sharing a small apartment with two girls, waiting tables to pay the bills. After a gap year, she tried college but was too distracted to sit still. Maggie's friend, Alex, hooked her up with a job at an ad agency downtown. Her life was gaining momentum. She took up smoking, then quit, then started again. At the agency, she felt wanted, needed, and smart. Her love of puns served her well. She was promoted several times and took to her job with great pride. A colleague at the agency introduced Maggie to Gadly, which led to a job offer in Nashville. She was hesitant to take a job out of town. But her new boyfriend — whom we'll meet later — convinced her this was the new beginning she wanted. Several hundred miles between Maggie and her parents was enough distance to buffer their complicated relationship. She'd tolerate the holidays back home knowing there was an escape route.

Moving out of town creates the uneasy task of deciding what to take with you. Moving can either be a time to lighten the load or a time to carry stubborn boxes of stuff we think we must keep. Maggie held on to trinkets from her grandmother. Other things, such as journals, represented the person she used to be. Anything ticking that box was given away or discarded. She chose, instead, to focus on the person she'd become. Her sky was opening, and she grabbed hold of it with the eagerness of a child.

2

Fall from Grace or a Graceful Fall

Dan Benchman comes from a well-to-do family whose father is an economist and former president of the Federal Reserve Bank of Chicago. The elder Benchman is a managing partner at the hedge fund North & Co— Gadly's client, and he has plans for his son to gain what he considers real-life experience before handing him the keys to the world. This relationship led to Dan's position working for Gadly in Nashville. Dan was on his way to playing pro ball, but the dream finished hard with a shoulder injury. In high school, Major League teams scouted him. A left-handed pitcher with an unhittable combination of power and control—the boy possessed a vanishing curveball that left hitters looking for the giant hole in their bats. But Dan ruined his shoulder in a motorcycle accident on a slippery side street in Evanston, north of Chicago. He rounded the corner to avoid a car cruising past a stop sign. The rear wheel gave way against the slick road, throwing him from the motorcycle, shoulder first onto the hard pavement. He slid for half a block before the curb stopped him cold. A year of surgeries and rehabilitation followed, but Dan couldn't take back his game. The fastball was slower and off the mark. The curveball hung where it used to disappear. Young sluggers rocked him, and he rarely made it through the lineup. The scouts moved on, as did Dan's love for the game. He walked away from baseball to focus on school, studying politics at the University of Chicago. There was always Dad's money to fall back on.

Baseball connected Dan to his grandfather. They had a common language in the lore of the game. His grandfather explained, with baseball, no one needs to tell you about greatness—they show you. Dan never played catch with his father, who was reliably busy. His grandfather, a Korean War veteran named Arthur Benchman, took Dan to his first Cubs game. The old vet drove him to Little League practice and on the way home, stopped at 7-Eleven for baseball cards and candy. Arthur didn't speak about the war or explain what caused him to walk with a limp. On driving home from the diamond, Dan studied his grandfather's hands. They showed ghosts of strength, but now they shook. Arthur held to a romantic view of baseball and translated that to life. A larger lesson was attached to each talk. His advice always transcended the subject, and he taught Dan to play the long game, even when it felt impossible.

Dan was twenty years old when his grandfather died. The pancreatic cancer was too much. It moved through the soldier's body, erasing dignity, before taking the life.

Arthur never saw Dan play after the accident. Too weak from cancer to leave the house though Dan visited — still in his uniform — to talk about the game. Dan talked about his struggles. Arthur told stories about Mickey Mantle—the greatest hurt player of all time. Imagine what The Mick would've done with two good legs.

These talks were inspiring and depressing. His grandfather meant well with tales of the greats but who could live up to a baseball god? Dan's arm wouldn't do what his heart wanted. Arthur, again, reminded Dan of the importance of playing the long game. He had to learn to walk away from baseball with dignity—the way Arthur walked away from the Marines, hobbled from the war. He taught Dan to take the hard lessons in life and recondition them into fuel for the future.

Arthur analogized baseball, explaining how great hitters struck out early in the game, waiting for the right time to strike.

Dan was confused by this.

"Why would someone take a third strike on purpose?"

"Because you're looking for the tics. How he tips his pitches. An early strikeout doesn't matter much. Strikeouts come with a cost. They take more pitches. Wears the arm down. Next time up, with a runner in scoring position, you're ready. Like a caged animal. Hungry, like an animal. The ball looks bigger to you now. Like a fucking balloon. You got'm on the ropes,

Danny. You see the body language change with a curve ball. Maybe it's the way his middle finger is on the seam or the way he licks his lips before he throws it. You know he hates pitching from the stretch. The early at-bats teach you everything you need to know. Play the long game. And when it's time, *crush* the motherfucker." Arthur smiled, accenting his pleasure by placing an unlit pipe between his lips. The lip of the pipe, pock-marked by nervous teeth.

These lessons stayed with Dan, and throughout his life they served him well. On difficult days, he remembered how Mickey Mantle ran around the bases on one good leg. Dan banked the setbacks as motivation for pushing through college and through his professional life.

After college, Dan moved to Nashville with his partner, Michael—a photographer. The young couple bought a house on the east side of town in a hipster neighborhood—a gentrified area filled with young, bearded professionals and expensive coffee. Murphy's opened a new location in East Nashville, across the street from Mickey's record store—whose survival depends on convincing the public to pay twenty-five bucks for a single wax disc instead of accessing the whole of recorded history on their phones for free. Dive bars and pawnshops dot the landscape alongside boutique stores selling clothes that will cost you one month's car payment. The neighborhood feels bohemian and safe, like a suburban strip mall overlayed with a sepia filter where diversity is gotten good and hard as people sleep at bus stops near others resting inside million-dollar homes.

Dan writes the talking points for Gadly. When a project needs public support, Dan finds the words. Gadly put Dan in charge of a development project bringing jobs to a working-class area. Michael pushed back, asking Dan why some neighborhoods are filled only with low-wage jobs and apartment buildings. These jobs don't pay enough to afford a mortgage. And the only living options are rentals. How can a family leave that cycle? Addicted to clichés—Dan repeats to Michael that politics is messy. The work Gadly is doing is good. "In the long run. You'll see," Dan said.

An idealist, Dan hasn't yet become that with which he fights. He believes in the talking points. It's why he's good at selling them.

In contrast, while studying politics in Chicago, the debates were hypothetical. How does one react when faced with real power? When the olive branch of success accompanies a caveat of loose ethics, can it be resisted? The desire to be something special often lies root in corruption. Try anything once. These truisms repeat so often they're almost meaningless. But things are commonplace for a reason. Maybe it's a flaw in the human condition since we are the only species to know there's an end date. Ambition is a desperate race against the clock. Grasping for legacy. And with legacy comes our best chance, our only chance at immortality.

Ambition is the rocket we use against the gravity of death's grip. And collateral damage — unfortunate as it is — fuels the upward progression. We climb on top of the poor souls who, through dumb evolutionary luck, missed the lottery.

Dan and Maggie's shared office is down the narrow hall from Gadly. The hallway walls are covered with framed black-and-white portraits of Gadly and various political leaders, including former presidents.

Stopping to look at the photographs, Dan imagined he was the subject. One day he'll own a company, he thought, trading the lights of the baseball diamond for the diaphanous glow of press admiration in his adopted city. The manually operated scoreboard at Wrigley Field saw history and was history. Just like the people in these photographs. Dan wanted to be a porter of history.

It tickled the same itch he once had for the game. Before his injury, he had nerves of steel. He thrived when the stakes were high. The guts it took to throw a pitch, on a full count, down and outside with the game on the line knowing his opponent couldn't resist the bait. That's how Dan felt about working big accounts for Gadly. He treated less glamorous clients with the same zeal. Remembering the sagacious words of his grandfather—train like you fight. Working at a chain restaurant account was like throwing simulated innings. He needed to hit his spots in preparation for the time when the game counted.

Dan was methodical—a wily player with an approachable exterior. He'd gut you with a smile. An efficient hunter, taking what he needs, and neatly discarding the rest. Friend is a loose term, and Dan refused the limitations of rigidity. Others will argue he lacked conviction and possessed no core values apart from winning. But there are no ties in baseball. He's been groomed to play the long game, knowing that even a long game ends with a winner and a loser. His destiny, he believed, was with the former, and he'd do whatever is necessary to avoid being the latter. People don't remember Mickey Mantle only because he was wounded. They remember him because, though injured, he won. Dan saw his story in the same light. A promising baseball career, cut short, is only compelling if he achieves greatness despite his dead arm. With any other outcome, there wouldn't be a story worth telling.

Maggie got along fine with Dan. The casual conversations between them were trivial and mundane, though he was fond of provoking her into debate. Dan held deep seated insecurities when he was around Maggie. She was unwilling to lower her values— stubbornly moral, and this ate at him.

Thinking there's an opening, he blindly shoots through it like he's cornered a maimed target. A typical exchange went something like this:

"Where do you go to church?" Dan asked,

unrelated to anything.

"I don't."

"Why not? Are you an atheist?"

"I'm not the religious kind."

"Not the religious kind. That's condescending."

"I don't mean it that way. I have so much work in front of me, please."

Maggie was hoping this would end the conversation; however, Dan, clueless to social cues, kept pushing.

"How can you *not* believe in God?"

"Which one?"

"What?"

"Which god are you asking me about?" Maggie was now beginning to enjoy the exchange.

"The real God. The others are myths."

"So, you can understand the mind of an atheist. You only believe in one more God than I do." Maggie said.

Dan paused with his mouth open while he juggled sweet reason and superstition. He felt like he was staring at Rubik's cube, thinking there must be some way to put the colors right.

Maggie continued. "I don't want to argue with you about religion. Believe what you want. Who gives a fuck."

"You speak with such certainty. I guess that's my problem with atheists—they speak with the certainty of a fundamentalist," Dan said. He had moved on to debating a point Maggie wasn't making. His fondness for straw-man arguments annoyed her, and she waved him off and returned to work. Dan's phone rang; he stepped out to take the call.

3

Despairing With Dignity

Maggie's closest colleague at work is Caitlin Cheney, the dedicated accountant. Caitlin is an attractive woman in her mid-forties, curious and smart. Her husband, Charlie, grew up with Gadly. He's an executive in the business of pharmaceuticals. The two were beneficial to each other. Gadly had the political capital and Charlie found the money. Charlie and Caitlin were opposites, and Maggie wondered what attracted them to each other in the first place. Charlie's naked ambitiousness seemed at odds with Caitlin's patience and grace. A luncheon, in Charlie's mind, was a time for business. He bragged about the number of deals he'd closed before dessert. His wife saw dining as a time to slow down and savor.

Caitlin was a math major in college, but learning she was pregnant, dropped out the summer before her final year. Charlie and Caitlin married quickly to keep peace with their parents. But the baby was born dead. The Cheney's never recovered emotionally from the loss. They named her Rebecca. Charlie threw himself into work and Caitlin started an accounting business from home—she was always good with numbers, finding poetry in the language of math. She began assisting Gadly, helping balance his books. Caitlin was instrumental in the company's success. The spreadsheet was her musical score. Within the numbers, she could see the scope of the entire enterprise. She helped Gadly make wise decisions and gave caution to his impulses and impatience. A few years back, Caitlin had taken a break from work, and it was then that things went south for Gadly. He misspent money, and alienated clients, creating a vacuum now filled by less profitable accounts, like Murphy's fake Irish pub. After a year of this, he begged her to return, and she agreed. It didn't take long to turn Gadly's mess around. The first step was to let loose of Murphy's. She told him he needed to act like a diamond if he wanted to be one. He always listened to her.

After Rebecca's death, Charlie took to drinking. It was a junk cure that only drove the two apart. The listless marriage provided a sameness they found comforting. The dull repetition worked as an emotional elixir offsetting their terrible loss. Charlie's drunkenness didn't affect his work, and he'd only take to the bottle after business hours. He was a prodigious marketing executive who'd grown numb to the world, and his torpefied existence created a shield against the stress of a fast-paced profession. Caitlin, on the other hand, spent hours in the room they prepared for Rebecca. She'd rearrange the — now unneeded —

bedroom and compulsively straighten blankets over the rocking chair she planned for nursing her daughter. Charlie looked on from the hallway, as she swayed with eyes closed reciting *Goodnight Moon* in a whisper. He didn't say a word.

Caitlin was kind and reliable around the office. Her blonde bob hairdo framed her face. Stylish and classy, the symmetry of her dress matched the exactness of her computations. A mathematician, Caitlin was the smartest person in the building. She and Maggie shared a love of old Hollywood, Patsy Cline, and cars.

During hellish episodes when it was time to purchase a new car, the dealer would bypass Caitlin and only speak to Charlie, who could barely find the gas tank. Part of the experience was Caitlin redirecting the dealer to her. She's buying a car. Don't speak to my husband about this. He doesn't know a damn thing about cars.

On the days when Gadly left the office after a stress tantrum — aimed in anyone's direction — Caitlin and Maggie bonded over film noir and Paris in the 1950s. Caitlin recalled lines from *Rififi* and Maggie gushed over Claude Sylvain's style.

They'd meet at Maggie's apartment for a girl's night of old French films, take-out, and red wine. Wine stains on the *Hemmings*. Though she smiled most of the time, Maggie could see the darkness hiding behind Caitlin's eyes. She'd only spoken of Rebecca on a few occasions and didn't show tears when retelling her tragedy. Maggie admired Caitlin's courage but felt sorry for her pang of loss. Maggie has an instinct for absorbing the pain of others. She held Caitlin as a kindred spirit, drenched in sorrow, and willing herself to carry on.

Caitlin's brilliance came with a cost. She's tech-challenged, and Maggie, with patience, assisted her daily with the printer. Though Maggie's paycheck was never on time, she saw Caitlin as above reproach. She admired her objection to technical modernity; its cold, hard, plastic automation, standing in contrast to her warm, soft touches. As endearing as that may be, Maggie preferred to avoid the maddening cat-and-mouse game of chasing Caitlin's fluid pay schedule, or better put, non-schedule.

Caitlin has a complicated past. A childhood of neglect that is at odds with her attentiveness. Her mother suffered from depression and medicated her condition by abusing pills. A part of Caitlin resented Charlie's professional life for this reason. She saw in her mother the real-time effects of the industry. Because she had a front-row view of her husband's dealings, she witnessed the emphasis of profits over care. Her mother put a face to a system of addiction—a system prioritizing symptoms over causes. She recognized this in Charlie's politics as well. Her mother, like many people, was doped with high hopes and left abandoned by empty promises. Charlie argued he was in the business of saving lives. He saw nothing wrong with self-dealing if done in the service of the public good. Caitlin was confident a fair portion of Charlie's money had blood on it. Her mother was one of the victims—dying of a drug overdose before the age of forty. OxyContin took the pain away.

Caitlin's father was a man of many women. He justified his infidelity by his wife's condition and his stressful work managing hedge funds. Though the work yielded money and women, he felt the emptiness of a life spent plundering, which left him on his knees at night, alone in a hotel room. As it was, he loved his daughter. He bought her expensive gifts on his travels. Caitlin clung to these gifts as treasure only to discover they were a replacement for an absent father. Her aunt raised her and influenced her. Through the encouragement of Aunt Odette, she read classic literature and learned the arts of camp and fashion. She learned etiquette; how to be both soft and firm—she learned to be poised. Caitlin still wears Odette's pearl earrings.

Odette encouraged Caitlin, "People spend their lives spectating others doing things. Be the one doing the doing. The only life worth living is one that is *lived*."

Exhortations like these became mantras Caitlin carried through difficult times.

Odette took her shopping for her first bra. Becoming comfortable in her body took some time. She would arrive, nurtured by her father's sister. Rebecca's birth and death certificates read: *Rebecca Odette*

Cheney.

The two drifted apart over the years. Nothing wrong between them; only the progression of lives moving in opposite directions. Caitlin watched Odette fall in love and move to rural France, where she settled into a quiet life as an amateur painter. Odette was older when she married. The phrase some use is: later in life. Later being arbitrary; it wasn't too late for Odette because that's how long it took for her to find her lover. And what care does time have with the subjective calendars of others? Finn, her beau, was a man of wealth and high education. His family held real estate in several countries, and he had the luxury to live anywhere. Odette met Finn at an art gallery in New York. A mutual friend set them up. Caitlin saw her off at the airport, and that was the last time they spoke. Caitlin watched with tears as Odette and Finn boarded a plane to a new life in France.

Caitlin pictured Odette in France, drunk with kisses, under the yellow sun, as she painted by a still lake. She was Caitlin's North Star. It's why she holds a wine glass as she does—savoring little moments before they're gone. Never in a rush with the glow of confidence. Caitlin mentored Maggie in this way, although she already had innate beauty. Maggie's sophistication wasn't born from a wealthy class. She arrived at style from modest beginnings. Maggie was a ship surviving the competing storms of an angry father and sick mother.

From behind, Caitlin would arrange Maggie's long red hair into a bun and say, "Wear your hair up, dear; you have a lovely neck. Show it off."

Maggie smiled. These little episodes gave her confidence. Caitlin acted like the mother Odette replaced. And Maggie found a mother figure in her.

A change in fortune reached the company. Gadly instructed Maggie to take the lead on a new project dealing with a shakeup at City Hall. Keeping her dark on the details was crucial to avoid leaks. Caitlin said Charlie was involved too. He hadn't slept in days, and the two cell phones he kept rang all the time. Charlie was to introduce Gadly to a man named George Davies. Davies — the former vice mayor — is an associate of Charlie's in a business Maggie didn't understand— something to do with housing and transporting pharmaceuticals. It sounded complicated by design which made Maggie uneasy. Dan was acting as a liaison between City Hall and the company. The responsibility made him feel important.

Gadly was jubilant. When Charlie brought something to him, it was always big. Gadly's talents rested in his ability to balance competing power structures. Charlie would connect private and public entities and Gadly tidied the messaging. If an initiative wasn't popular, it was on Gadly to make it so. Whatever was happening at City Hall was going to be disruptive. Charlie would guide the ship while Gadly convinced the public that the glacier the city was heading for would be an island of prosperity. This involved planting favorable stories in the press using strategic leaks. Gadly knew the journalists sympathetic to the cause, and he'd manipulate them to publish glowing pieces by trading information. If you hit the wave just right, you can bend public perception in your favor because most people are too busy with their daily lives to keep up with the details. Distracted by a steady diet of social media and TV, the commoners' attention span has only enough gas for the headline. The article leaves them stranded on the road, distracted by fast food and bullshit. An uninformed public is easy to manipulate. They've done the heavy lifting for you by knowing little about how their government works.

Solving problems is a complicated business. Too complicated for most people to understand. Instead, you abandon nuance, divide the issues down to a war between the good guys and the bad guys—a lucrative trade in the business of Us versus Them. Groups of people are defined as monoliths—usually by people outside the group, setting up a collision course with populism and grievance.

The final and most crucial ingredient is the demagogue—a savior-like figure used to build a personality cult. Scrupulous men like Charlie Cheney and George Davies were masters at this game.

4

A Novel Spy

Maggie shares a downtown apartment with her boyfriend, Liam Harrison—a writer. A wealthy developer owns the space and leases it to the young couple at a reasonable price. Liam met him last year at an upscale bar where he once worked. It was a joint Liam used to sustain himself prior to his first book deal. From behind the counter, he made friends with everyone from sad and lonely drunks to CEOs—often the same people. He'd chat with his thirsty audience for hours, studying and cataloging them for future characters.

Liam has a talent for finding luck. A master at landing on his feet, he convinced the high-rise developer to lease the pricey apartment at a discounted rate. In return, Liam agreed to work off the balance, helping around the building performing maintenance such as painting or replacing light fixtures. His end of the agreement lasted only a month before Liam gave up the gig. The developer was indifferent because Liam continued to ply him with drinks to medicate his friendless existence at the top. This man — Liam knew his name at some point — had relied upon himself, and only himself, to rise atop the heap. When he arrived, he looked around to see there was no one else in sight. At first, this pleased him. He was exclusive. But it came to him that exclusivity is also a subtraction, a restricted space from others.

Now on top of a mountain of success, he feared losing it all. With paranoia comes more subtraction. Fewer people around you, fewer opportunities for losing hard-fought gains. Friends only came around for money, so friends were no longer allowed. A lover may prize his riches above all else, so that door was closed. To avoid temptation, he secured the gate with the deadbolt of individualism, thus cementing his solitude—a moneyed hermit who flowered his decaying soul with paid sex, possessions, and booze.

Liam's first book, *L'Affaire Twin*, was picked to be made into a TV series on a major streaming service. It's a spy novel set in England in the 1970s. The Cold War-era plot centers on Peter Tufton, an intelligence officer who suspects his superior is a Soviet mole. Tufton is leading Operation Landowne, an allied collaboration built to disrupt a collection of moles embedded inside the highest levels of British intelligence. When the secret location of a safe house is revealed, Tufton realizes his wife, Rosa—an Italian expat, has become romantically involved with the mole, and they are now plotting against him. The disclosure of the safe house, located in Prague, was a plan to murder Peter. Peter outwits his enemies by leaving instructions with a Polish operative to surround the building. Rosa attempts to distract Peter with seduction while her lover, the mole, stabs him in the back. Unbeknownst to Rosa, Peter used his twin brother, Phillip, to stand in. Peter, an expert sniper, is across the street on top of a neighboring building and removes the mole with a single clean shot. They arrest Rosa, and the entire affair sets off an international panic as the world realizes a network of sleeper agents are now embedded deep in Western governments.

Liam's best friend is Jack Howe, an A-list actor starring in and directing the spy series. They met in high school in suburban Kansas City. Jack was raised in Lexington and moved north with his family at age nine. His father was a jazz musician who worked a day job in an auto parts plant. Jack's mother, Rita, was a public-school teacher. She also wrote children's books and was active in community politics. She'd engage local officials, encouraging them to add a stop sign or lobby on behalf of the neighborhood for sidewalks. Amis Howe, Jack's father, was a skilled guitarist, and in Lexington, played multiple times a week with his band Stella, and the Bell Tones. A modest job promotion and transfer brought the family to Kansas City. Once settled in Missouri, he never found another band but often played outside on the back porch as neighbors gathered to listen when the weather was nice.

Jack was a natural talent at sports — any sport — and was uninterested in learning how to play an instrument. He sang well, a skill he inherited from his mother who sang old jazz standards around the house. The family joked that Jack "came out singing." He was an easy performer who loved the attention. As it happened, Jack could dance too. As a young boy, he'd boogie to his father's guitar playing during those summer concerts while Rita sang along. The Howe family made friends in Kansas City, and it didn't take long for KC to feel at home. Jack had the looks, the wit, and the charm. Neighbors swooned over the boy, predicting he'd one day be famous. Jack bought the hype and planned to leave for Hollywood the day he graduated high school. And so, he did.

Liam and Jack became like brothers in school. They were inseparable, and together, got up to no good while trying to navigate adolescence. Like brothers, they fought. A lot. Even on a busy city street, the volume of their arguments would rise above the noise of traffic. Jack knew he could hurt Liam and often did. He wasn't sadistic, but his insecurity of Liam tugged at his core. In high school, Liam's girlfriend cheated on him with Jack. He arrived one afternoon to apply his signature triplet knock on Jack's window, prompting him outside. Through the glass, Liam saw his girlfriend, Caroline, lying with Jack in the basement bedroom of the Howe's split-level—watching them laugh like they'd forgotten he existed. The boys fought about it, then resigned themselves to laughing off the ridiculous episode.

Liam loved and resented his best friend. He felt like the universe was looking out for Jack. A mixture of superstition and envy occupied his thoughts, leaving him feeling guilty. The guilt was a motivating force for Liam to forgive Jack each time he felt betrayed. Jack knew this and didn't fail to use it to his advantage.

The two leave for London in a few days and will be on location assisting the screenwriters with the TV series. Jack arrived from New York, where he was filming an Art Deco commercial for *Cassandre Parfum* as the company's global ambassador. The company is named after a famous French painter. Born in Kharkiv, died by suicide in Paris.

Jack is staying with Liam and Maggie to work on the script until they depart for England. Maggie doesn't like it when Jack comes around because he finds little ways to hurt Liam, a soft target for his best friend.

In New York, Jack was naked on the bathroom floor of a luxury apartment. One leg over the other, cubist abs selling an expensive fragrance.

In Nashville, a steady diet of take-out food and empty liquor bottles are abandoned alongside Jack's etiquette. He's a bad house guest who uses flattery to maintain Maggie's patience—*He loves the novel. Maggie is smart and pretty.* And so on. Jack flirts with the idea of buying a place here; Maggie prays he won't.

He pounds on about how nice it would be to own a cabin on a few acres, speaking as though she and Liam live on a prairie because an ocean doesn't border their city. Thinking he's exotic because he eats sushi, Liam reminds him you can buy it in a gas station. Lately Jack has become prone to conspiracy thinking. He'll bring up nonsense about vaccines or something another actor has told him about JFK's assassination. Liam tried to explain the facts, but as the crackpot theories mounted, he lost patience and changed the subject. Jack's recent obsession is pushing fad diets. He's concerned about what goes in his body—pausing to sink a Scotch. Forget reason, that's not what got him here.

It wasn't all a butting of heads. The three stayed up late drinking and sharing old stories. The same tales they repeated to each other over the years. There was the time back in Kansas City when they made their way through several bars, and at the end of the night, walking to the hotel, Jack spotted a sidewalk sign and assured everyone he could clear it. With a running start a few yards away, Jack leaped, only to come down hard, smashing his balls straight onto the unforgiving structure. There he lay, an A-list actor, writhing around on a Kansas City sidewalk, with his pelvis in his chest. He moaned in agony but laughed hysterically. The story never got old.

On another ridiculous occasion — without the dignity of intoxication as an excuse for stupidity — Liam and Jack decided to take off their clothes and run streaking through a fast-food drive-thru. As they made their way around the lighted menu, the naked pair spotted Liam's mom in the pickup line. They darted for the shrubs and landed, bare-assed, in a crowd of thorny bushes. The duo waited for Liam's mom to pull away as the branches tore at their flesh. Bleeding and second-guessing the stunt, the wounded nudes rounded up their clothes and limped home. Maggie reveled in the misadventures of the two boys. She was grateful for the prudence of her younger years, for there wasn't a time where she jumped naked into a pile of shrubs. For Liam and Jack, two friends without siblings, the pair found the brother they never had.

In high school, Liam encouraged Jack to try out for the school play. Jack was focused on sports at the time but was nursing a season-ending injury. He landed the role of Mark Antony in the school's production of *Julius Caesar*. The play changed his life. He abandoned sports and made his way to the West Coast. He worked as a waiter for a year and a half, between commercials and modeling gigs. Then came the sitcom that made him famous.

He was cast as a lawyer named Bruce Hunt in a TV show. Hunt's wife was wrongly accused of murdering their son. The crooked district attorney trumped up the allegations to ruin Hunt's reputation as payback for corruption charges leveled against him. The child's murder was a random, criminal act, and Hunt's wife, a disgraced judge, became the primary suspect. The show had a cult following online even after the studio canceled it. 'Brucers,' as his fans were known, pursued conspiracy theories around the show's abrupt cancellation. The series was a failure, but Jack became an icon with a fanbase. Leading movie roles came and up went his star. Like with sports, Jack was a natural with a way of manipulating situations, tweaking the emotions of others in his favor. Acting provided a sweet spot for him to earn money with a trade he perfected long ago.

Liam was proud of his friend's success and never turned down Jack's invitations to movie premieres. He toured Hollywood with his friend showing off how he no longer had to wait in line for things. Liam was enamored by it all. They'd hang out at the beach during the day and wind up at an elite restaurant eating exotic food by night. Jack spent the night impersonating a playboy, but Liam knew better. Jack was good at façades, but his friend could see the cracks. In honest moments, Jack was romantic. His life was full of flair, but he longed for the calming security of being cozy on the couch, watching a movie with a lover. His filming and travel schedule made it tough to find someone to love. He'd cure loneliness with a fellow actor on the set. A little romp in the trailer. A long-term relationship wasn't in the cards, but the one-night stands did provide a human touch. It wasn't only about the sex. He needed the contact, and casual sex provided him with a band-aid to cover the hole in his heart. But Jack wanted something more. For that, he would have to wait.

5

A Path Best Avoided

Maggie returned to the office late Friday night because she'd forgotten a client folder she needed for work over the weekend. The lights were on upstairs, and she assumed Dan must have left in a hurry. Reaching the top of the stairs, Maggie heard drunken laughter coming from Gadly's office. She knew Gadly's sound, but the woman's voice Maggie couldn't place—though it possessed a familiarity. Gadly lost his wife to illness years ago and didn't speak of a private life. He ignored flirtations from women at parties. It was always business.

Maggie crept down the hall, and around the corner, she could see into his office. To her surprise, she found Caitlin, on top of Gadly, straddling him as they reached for each other's bodies in desperation. He lifted her skirt, moved her underwear to the side like he was peeling off alternating layers of taboo and innocence. Peeling away innocence to find the taboo. Or was it the other way around?

It was sex as consciousness. Not only about the body. Their bodies were working together, sure, but there was more to it. A married woman having an affair. A man sleeping with his best friend's wife. On the surface this is objectively bad. A scandal. Let the judgement begin. But right or wrong doesn't always fit. Sometimes it's a false choice. So, *on the surface* may be like reading the cover but not the book. It was all crashing inside Maggie's brain as she stared at the scene in front of her.

Caitlin brought Gadly to her chest. Why did it seem motherly? Oedipal. The scene brought back those old French films. In a low-lit Victorian office, this episode was something she hadn't experienced but was something she should have expected in the center of a *beau monde*. In awe of Caitlin's beauty, she stood still watching what her eyes couldn't believe. She snapped out of her pause and returned to the reality of the scandal.

The two, horned up like vines, didn't notice a cataleptic Maggie stilled in the doorway. She almost choked in shock but covered her mouth before any sound could escape her lips. She backed away through the hall, avoiding the creaks she was familiar with and tiptoed down the stairs not daring to breathe. Maggie's tall heels were not designed to be clandestine. The whole point of the heel is to be noticed. Each step on the aged wooden floors threatened to give her away. The more carefully she stepped, the louder she sounded. Her heart was beating like it was trying to escape her chest. It was difficult to breathe, and she thought she'd never get out before Gadly and Caitlin noticed they weren't alone. The scene started to feel like a dream where the hallway grows longer the closer you get to the door. An endless loop of steps toward an exit you will never reach. Finally, she did reach the door and with the door came another obstacle. Now she tried her best to open it like a spy escaping, minimizing the sound of rusted hinges. She was dizzy with anxiety.

Maggie stepped out of the building, and the cold air revived her lungs. She leaned against the brick façade and took a moment to collect herself. Her back was soaking with sweat, and her dress felt suffocating. The street was as quiet as the dead and the full moon's light added to the peculiarity of the situation. She crossed the street to her car, leaving the office without retrieving the folder. She couldn't wait to tell Liam what had happened.

At home, Maggie pushed through the door in a panic. She spoke without breath when she found Liam and Jack, already drunk, sharing an old childhood story. With Scotch burning through their bodies, they recalled the time they skipped class and came across Tony Dribble pouring deer piss into the school's HVAC unit. The high school had been smelling like stale urine for a week, and no one had a clue what was happening. On the way back to class, they were stopped in the hall by their biology teacher, Sister Larrett, a former nun who dropped the habit but kept the sister part. Jack diverted her attention around the corner to where Tony was dumping piss into the school's heating and cooling system. The school suspended Tony, but it would be days before the smell of urine was cleared from the air. Liam and Jack were drunk and laughing while Maggie took on a serious tone.

"Liam, I just saw Gadly and Caitlin."

"Where?" Liam said.

"At the office. She was…"

"She was what?" Liam could see she was alarmed but he was confused and drunk.

"Kissing and—"

Liam jumped up. "*Caitlin*?"

"They were on his office couch."

"I thought she was married." Liam was shocked and excited by the news.

"She is."

Jack intervened. "Who are Gadly and Caitlin?"

"Richard Gadly is Maggie's boss."

"Caitlin and Dick."

"This isn't funny, Jack. Caitlin's husband connected George Davies to Gadly. This whole thing could get messy, fast." Maggie was beside herself.

"I thought they were bringing corruption charges against Davies," Liam said. "Gadly is going to work with that grifter?"

"Mayor Binks has resigned. I don't know all the details, but George Davies is running to replace him in a special election in August and Gadly has been hired to help with the campaign."

Maggie kicked off her heels, took Liam's freshly poured drink from his hand, kissed his cheek, and headed to the couch. She couldn't stop thinking about it. If Charlie found out Caitlin was sleeping with Gadly, not only would it kill the new deal with George Davies, but this could be the thing to snap Charlie out of his drunken stupor. Who knows what he might be capable of in a desperate condition.

Maggie woke up early the next morning. Liam stayed in bed and Jack slept on the couch. She wasn't sure how to confront Gadly about Caitlin. Or even if it was a good idea to do so. She couldn't risk losing her job. Liam hadn't received his advance yet, so she was covering most of the bills. I need to clear my head, she thought. She got dressed, put in her earbuds, and went for a run.

An hour later, on her way home, Maggie's phone rang. It was Gadly.

"We closed the George Davies account."

"Wonderful news. I didn't realize things would move so quickly".

"I wasn't expecting it either. It's almost like something magical happened last night, and *boom*— here we are."

"Last night indeed."

"What did you say? I think your phone is cutting out."

"I said I'm thrilled about the new account. I can't wait to get started on it."

"Well, be ready. Davies will be in the office Monday morning. I need you there early. You must beat him to the office and make sure everything is perfect."

"Will Dan be there?"

"No, I've sent him to DC. He returns on Wednesday."

"I'll be ready."

"We are back in the game."

Maggie hung up the phone. Her heart was now racing. It was too late to approach Gadly about his affair with Caitlin. But she needed to find out if they were to see each other again. Maggie knew having George Davies around the office would only complicate things.

Charlie Cheney was instrumental in getting the state to drop the fraud and money laundering charges against Davies. The schemes took place in the public health sector, with Charlie. They manipulated billing codes inside pharmacies to submit fraudulent claims. These claims for medications weren't prescribed by doctors or given to patients. Fake wholesale companies were used to wire funds. When the invented proceeds outpaced the available cash, their associates transferred money back from the sham companies. After moving money through associates, they used the actual proceeds to invest in real estate as Nashville's market boomed. The web was so complicated that Charlie's fingerprints disappeared. Davies smeared his involvement with a wall separating the man from the crime. He stayed protected by the unbreakable shield of plausible deniability. There was no scenario where a jury would ever convict him. The pair walked away as clean as the money they had washed. They also defrauded taxpayers by securing government contracts to finance these crimes. Charlie held massive influence over the Metro Council as he was responsible for most of the council members being there in the first place. Many of their businesses and property investments were part of this scheme. Cheney and Davies were safe. It's like nuclear powers avoiding war by mutually assured destruction. No one in their right mind is going to press the button.

The city was growing because of Gadly's work luring big businesses to Nashville. Like where Dan Benchman lives, neighborhoods were being gentrified using laundered money generated by the crimes. Charlie had convinced Gadly that he was bringing the big players back. George Davies would be like a magnet, drawing in powerful clients from around the world. This collective would be Gadly's path back to the big leagues. He was a pawn in this chess match and had no idea because he was distracted by flattery, private jets, and now, Caitlin. The one question rattling around Maggie's head was this: *Is Caitlin in on the scheme, too?*

6

Liam and Jack in London

Liam and Jack arrived at Heathrow in the morning. The airport was loud with world travelers, and the two spent an hour and a half getting through customs. Jack killed time going over the script. He did most of the talking as Liam felt comatose from the overnight flight. Jack drank himself to sleep and dozed like a log for the entire journey. Now he was wide awake and eager for the work ahead. After collecting their bags, they grabbed breakfast, exchanged money, and headed for the car Jack had arranged for them. Despite the stiff leather seats inside the car, Liam closed his eyes and fell asleep in minutes. The interior smelled like old people, not smelly bodies but the smell of death drawing nearer. It was strong and stinky but not strong enough to keep Liam from sleeping. The drive east to London felt like an instant by the time Jack nudged him awake. They arrived at The Mill, a film & TV studio in central London. Jack had worked here before. Knew his way around. He knew his way around most places.

"We're not stopping by the hotel first?" asked

Liam. His eyes burned from exhaustion.

"No time for that, Shake. There's too much work to do." Jack repeated the nickname he had stuck on Liam in high school. Freshman year, each student had to stand up at their desk and speak a little about themselves. Talk about career goals. Liam said to the room of strangers that he wanted to be a writer.

Jack referenced Shakespeare by calling him Liam *Shake*. The class erupted at Liam's expense.

When the teacher called on Jack, he answered, "I want to be a professional wrestler." Jack's absurdity washed away Liam's embarrassment and the two became instant friends.

Jack used comedy to dull the knife of insecurity. He used it to disarm his opponents. His wit was artful, and it served him well. He seemed bulletproof and charmed his way out of difficult situations. Liam admired Jack's ability to brush off criticism. Liam's insecurities were debilitating. He was a shy and quiet friend, and Jack seemed to know no stranger. Jack appeared like a character on TV. One of those TV shows where the kids in high school look and act like they're in their twenties. The other kids prayed for death over a toilet bowl at parties, but Jack handled his drink *like a sir*. Most high school boys were nervous talking to girls. For Jack, these conversations flowed with ease. His confidence was infectious. You'd find him in the hallway chatting with the history teacher like they were old pals. Jack charmed his way from below average grades to average grades. Some kids are good at school. But that's where it ends. Jack had old wisdom. He knew nothing about the details of the American Revolution, but he knew *life*. Understood how things worked. A D- on dates and battle locations. Valedictorian on the fine art of manipulation. To get what you want. Get where you want to go. He saved himself, caught skipping class, by throwing old Tony Piss under the bus. Jack already knew how the real world worked.

Liam and Jack were lower-middle-class kids. Jack looked stylish in everything he wore, not because of money, but clothes hung on him in the right way. Liam lived in hand-me-downs. He was embarrassed by the ill-fitting clothing, and everything he wore seemed perversely out of style. Most kids don't appreciate the work it takes for their parents to raise them. It was expensive. As it is, at a certain age, kids do notice bad style. But the off branding wasn't the biggest problem. Liam's shoes were inherited from a cousin, so they'd formed to somebody else's feet. The used cleats were broken in all the wrong ways, a size too big, with the toes pointing toward the sun. The pleated pants hanging from his lower half gave the humiliated teen the appearance of a middle-aged dad balancing on two deflated, off-brand innertubes posing as shoes. Liam's cousin had linebacker thighs and a giant ass. The pants swallowed him whole. He looked like a rake dressed in a hot air balloon.

In his senior year, Liam saved enough money to

buy a pair of leather boots. He worked in the kitchen of a buffet style restaurant. Cooking alongside drug addicts and convicts, he made decent money for a teenager. The manager, a restaurant lifer in his forties, used to screw the hostesses in his Ford Bronco. Right there in the parking lot. The Bronco must have smelled of Salisbury steak and sex. The old man, a degenerate, had the odd habit of breathing inward through his nose when he spoke. The nose, abused by snorting crushed pills, ready to collapse at any moment. Most people end sentences with punctuation. A period. Anything. This guy would finish his thoughts with a long-inverted sniff.

With his buffet style restaurant money, Liam went shopping with Jack, and when they walked in the store, he spotted the boots under the display case light like he had found the Holy Grail. As the salesperson left to retrieve his size, Liam stood there admiring the display boot. With the correct size in hand, he slipped it on his foot and couldn't believe something could feel this good. It was the first time in his life he had worn a decent shoe. Liam admired the boot in a full-length mirror, shifting to observe his foot from multiple angles. He didn't care how much they cost—he would have traded a car for these stylish kicks.

Liam wore the leather boots outside of the store and would have swaggered down the street had he not been paranoid about scuff marks.

Jack decided on getting a tattoo that day. Neither he nor Liam had ever been inside a tattoo shop and were jarred by the obscure heavy metal music blasting through the speakers. It may have been a German band, but they weren't sure. The two suburbanites tried to act cool, as though they weren't out of place, but Liam's stiff, shiny boots gave the game away. Jack decided on a Capricorn sign to be forever etched onto his left forearm.

"You said astrology is bullshit," Liam said. He hoped to save his friend from a terrible mistake.

"It is. I just like the symbol, and it'll look better than stamping my birth month on my arm."

Jack had to wait an hour for his appointment, so he and Liam left to eat lunch, and that was enough time for a change of heart. The reversal was the right move because Jack would go on to film many shirtless scenes in his future career. He had a nice body, and it became a running joke in Hollywood for the director to find any excuse for Jack Howe to lose his shirt.

Jack on a boat. [Shirt off].

Jack to receive a critical phone call. [Lying in bed, shirtless].

Jack is told the bad guys are getting close. [Let's try another one without the shirt].

Speaking of shirtless boys, Liam lost his virginity at age seventeen to a girl called Alex—the same Alex who helped Maggie land a job at the ad agency in KC. Alex was the same age, but she wasn't a virgin. Like most boys at seventeen, he was excited, nervous, and awkward. Each time he hung out at Alex's house —

where her divorced mom was never around — they'd spend the afternoon exploring each other's bodies. All of it was new to him. Before Alex, he'd kissed a girl, but that's where his experience stopped. The fateful night happened on a weekend. Alex's mom was out for the night —which is a strange thing to say because her mom was never really 'in'— so a group of friends descended on her house for a party. The stoners and drinkers stood on opposite sides of the room, partitioned like the Jets and the Sharks. Liam and Alex were alone in her room, which already resembled a bedroom you might find in an adult's apartment. Liam's bedroom still had hints of childhood—like his baseball card collection or the crucifix his parents hung in his room, above the door frame. This room was not that. Alex wore heavy eyeliner and black clothing. She, too, wore boots, but hers were already scuffed. Liam thought there was a good chance Alex was probably born in her boots. As she touched him, he forced his mind anywhere but the soft hand now down his jeans. He wanted to act like he'd been here before, but it was clear he hadn't. Liam tried remembering Jack's sex advice. But Alex was in charge this night, so Liam did the wise thing and abandoned Jack's guidance.

After leaving the party, Jack's curiosity was killing him. He interrogated his best friend as they drove in search of fast food.

Jack began the questioning, "So, how was it?"

"It was... It just happened." Liam was embarrassed

though a smile had hardened on his face.

"But what happened *exactly*? How did it go down?"

"We were kissing in the dark. Well, not completely dark. Alex has lots of candles. Lots and lots of candles. A record was playing in the background. My mind wandered for a minute to the music. I think it was Bright Eyes. She put me on my back, climbed on top, and put me inside her. I think I went blind for a moment."

Jack was there as Liam was coming of age. Liam cared for Alex, and Jack guided him like a protective older brother.

"Did you wear a condom?"

"No. I had one in my wallet, but it all happened so fast. I forgot I had it on me. I didn't even take off my boots."

Jack laughed then went serious, "You gotta wear a rub, Liam. Don't forget next time. And take off your boots. It's rude to lay in bed with boots on."

A rare occasion where Jack gave good advice. Not just the part about responsible sex, but Liam's boots still weren't broken in, and he explained to Jack that both feet had fallen asleep during the scandalous episode. He had to lie back on the bed to pull up his pants because it felt like the crown of thorns were pushing into his feet when he tried standing. Far from being the worst part, Liam was also nursing a massive blister inflicted by the inflexible boots onto his right big toe. The reason for including these details is to drive home just how sloppy and awkward the entire affair was. Liam, a swain still wearing the boots that punished his feet, thinking of George Brett to avoid coming too quickly while losing his virginity to *Cassadaga*.

Liam thought about his prized George Brett rookie baseball card. They should have printed a George Brett rage card, he thought. *The Pine Tar Collection*. The picture, a photograph of George Brett — in 1983 — losing his shit on the umps because he got caught cheating. How dare they? Turn the card, where the stats usually live, over to find an explanation for the cheat. Liam loved 80s baseball. It was vintage to him. Back when baseball players did street drugs. Before the late 80s steroids. The players then had unkempt mustaches and tight pants. Now they wear relaxed pants with careful facial hair. But George Brett is royalty. Kansas City fucking royalty.

The thought experiment did not work.

Jack was the first to notice Liam's talent for writing. They sat side by side in English class, and Jack read an essay Liam wrote about Bob Dylan's biographical myths. Jack thought his friend's work read like a movie. He saw Liam's talent for writing poetry through prose. But the rhythm of his poetry was stretched across pages. Meter, hidden in the pace of his stories. Even his piece on Dylan had a kind of fiction to it. Poetry and prose. Myth and biography. Bob Dylan and Robert Zimmerman.

His English teacher, Mr Andrew, echoed these

words of encouragement. He connected Liam with a professor at Columbia University. Liam was undecided whether to pursue a school outside of Kansas City, though he did imagine leaving his hometown at some point in his life. His parents couldn't afford Columbia, but a combination of good grades and debt paved the way for Liam to study in New York.

Liam had always enjoyed writing, but this was the first time he had thought about it as a profession. All it took was someone noticing and reacting to his words. Writing is a lonely profession and it's not easy knowing whether something is good, or not. Jack's emotional connection helped, and Mr Andrew's intellectual relationship gave him confidence.

Dismissive voices still lived in Liam's head. But he resisted the urge to give in to his parents' cynicism.

He didn't realize it then, but what motivated Liam to write was his perception of how powerful words can be. Like many, his motivation was born from pain. His parents weren't supportive and looked on his writing as frivolous. They were not subtle people. The Harrisons preferred that he study law but instead, he chose to tell stories. They characterized their son as whimsical, and John, his father—a man beaten by the club of a hard-lived life, had long since surrendered to dark cynicism. Liam's mom, Anne, felt poetry was pretentious. Liam thought, perhaps she read bad poems. It's sad to think how much the Harrisons missed out on by spending their time wishing Liam to be something he wasn't. He erased hours alone in his bedroom, typing on the old manual machine he had purchased from a second-hand shop. Though he had a computer in his room, he preferred a tactile approach to composition. His early writing wasn't great and looking back, he's embarrassed reading through most of it. What does live in those naïve writings is a young boy trying to understand the human condition by telling stories. He read widely and wrote every day. Liam tried explaining to his father that he didn't *want* to be a writer—a writer is who he *was*.

John Harrison, flipping through a magazine, offered advice. "Son, most people don't end up working a job they like. Think I dreamed of working in a grocery store? There's no pie in the sky. And if you look up long enough, a bird is liable to shit on your face."

Liam thought the premise of this conversation was bullshit. He wouldn't dare give up on his dreams. Not at this age. Dream isn't the right word anyway. A dream, by definition, is an aspiration—an ideal. He saw writing as a craft—his craft. Liam didn't aspire to be a writer; he was already doing it—a distinction John and Anne Harrison missed. So, when they insisted on referring to his writing as a fanciful dream, his parents taught Liam a valuable lesson: his home wasn't the place for big ideas. He knew one day he'd have to leave it behind to move forward. Kansas City felt like a permanently grounded plane, and he was determined to get off the ground.

Liam wondered if his father had dreams of growing up. There weren't many photographs of John Harrison as a child. And children in those dusty photographs still looked old. Like they were born middle aged. John answered with anecdotes about Liam's grandparents and great-grandparents being practical people. Work was a utility. They shed romantic ideas after arriving in America. America *was* the romanticized ideal. A job is what keeps the ideal above water. A group of peasants coming to America didn't have the luxury of thinking about college or a fulfilling career. Liam's grandfather, having emigrated from Ireland, worked in a factory and his grandmother stayed at home raising kids. He was dealing with what life was like being an Irish Catholic in America. But he saw the new country as a land of opportunity, and his son, John, carried the torch a little farther. Though John's work in a grocery store was less taxing than the factories, it wasn't glamorous either. John flirted with community college after high school, but it didn't stick. He found a job where he earned more than his father did. His parents saw progress with Liam's opportunity for college. With a college degree, Liam could find work that wasn't toxic to his lungs, or at least he'd find a job that didn't require a name tag. Anything from that was being greedy. The trade-off is tuition debt but progress, like most things, comes with a cost. John was frustrated that his son couldn't see this or chose not to see it. Liam saw it another way.

The opportunities America offered, even as an

ideal, are only good if they are not wasted. Liam was grateful for the sacrifices of his grandparents and those who came before them—the names of whom he didn't know.

The names he didn't know. It bothered him. Liam wanted to know the characters and stories buried deep in his family's history. It wasn't an exercise in nostalgia. He could better understand himself if he understood his original story. Why weren't their stories told? His grandparents died before he was born, so he missed out on a lifetime of wisdom direct from their mouths. John and Anne didn't share much about their family histories. It upset Liam that the stories of people with so much life had vanished. He planned to dig up these metaphorical graves. It was like resurrecting the dead.

Liam imagined stories based on his ancestors. Brought to life to share and immortalize them. His father's lineage ran back to Ireland, with some immigrants in England, crammed in houses in Manchester, working construction jobs for cheaper wages than the locals. His mother's family was also from Manchester. They built canals. Then railways. Then roads. From peasants to laborers. From the working class in the old country to the middle class in the new country. Liam wanted to know the story of how it happened. It was the story of how *he* happened.

His character, Peter Tufton, is based on an Englishman — twin Englishmen — from his mother's side. Though his parents had little interest in family history, his mom's older sister, Aunt June, provided a library of information. She would be the first stop in his time travels back along the paternal Harrison and maternal Smith tracks home.

The books were Liam's window to the outside world. In the pages he met bohemian characters living in exotic places. Everything exciting going on in the world seemed to be happening outside of his hometown. Liam didn't want to spend his life reading about interesting things people were getting up to in other places; he wanted to experience it and dared to do so. The best way he knew to get there was to write. His earliest stories were reflections on Aunt June's family tales. The Peter Tufton character in *L'Affaire Twin* appeared in many narratives. Before Liam imagined Tufton as an intelligence officer, he was written as a soldier, grocery clerk, and in his earliest incarnation, a footballer. Though his profession and circumstances fluctuated with each plot Liam penned or typed, Peter Tufton was always the hero. June spoke in admiration of this ancestor, and she was an engaging storyteller herself. Liam wasn't sure how many of these stories were embellished or if they even happened at all. But it was a start on his journey to understand his family's story. To understand himself.

After spending hours with his aunt, Liam spent more hours banging out stories on his manual typewriter—though by college he had abandoned the vintage machine for the ease of a laptop. He'd begin with character sketches based on Aunt June's recollections. Reading through old letters passed along generations, Liam was struck by how much some people had to endure. One letter in particular spoke of a widow sending her children to an orphanage because she couldn't afford to care for them. In the letter, she explained that she was hoping to find work and raise money before her children were adopted, knowing if that happened, she'd never see them again. Liam was empathetic, but the old letters taught him to feel and write in a deeper way. He had a responsibility to honor these people. Without them, he wouldn't exist.

To his girlfriend's dismay, Liam's computer became a regular part of their landscape.

Alex lost patience with Liam.

"Are you going to sit there all day and write?"

"I'm almost finished. Five minutes, I promise."

He didn't keep his promise, and after growing bored with him, Alex would leave to meet friends. On some days, he'd meet up with them, but other days he carried on with his work. Time disappeared as he lost himself in invented stories.

There was a small club downtown offering spoken word readings on Thursday nights. It was called Knickers. After returning from college, Liam became a regular at the club. During his first reading, Liam was so full of panic he couldn't breathe. Maggie was there, and she loved hearing him read. She was nervous for him and swore she'd never get on stage to speak in front of an audience. Before the gig, he'd print handbills to hang around town promoting the event. He invited his mother, but she never showed. Liam was desperate for her approval, and Anne had no idea how her apathy gutted him.

The crowd at Knickers was a strange mix of artists and writers. People in bands. Overly manicured facial hair and sweaters. Some people forced big words into their vocabularies like they were rehearsing the 'Word of the Day' they received in their email that morning. Jack said it's a place where feminists got up and spoke about their tits as burdens. Liam just wanted to tell stories.

Liam's father was busy with work, and his schedule didn't allow time for poetry readings. John worked in produce. His co-workers talked about their kids' playing sports. Liam's writing sounded like a language he didn't speak. But Liam played sports too. He loved baseball and played for his high school team. Liam asked his dad to play catch, but John was either too tired or not in the mood. So, Liam would head out to the back yard alone, with his ball and glove, and throw the ball as high as he could, waiting underneath to retrieve the pop fly. Always thinking of a story, Liam imagined he was playing in the World Series. He'd recite the play-by-play while running down the ball in his back yard. The imaginary game was full of drama: a veteran player in his sunset years with a clutch hit or a wounded pitcher overcoming what should have been a career-ending injury to strike out the final batter. It was always bases loaded in the bottom of the ninth. He loved bringing hero myths to life.

Liam's game-saving catch might go something like this:

"Chip Gibson missed all last season, out after Tommy John surgery on his throwing arm. They said his return was impossible, but here he is, with the game on the line. The Royals are clinging to a one-run lead in the Highway 70 series against the St. Louis Cardinals. The sacks are jammed with a full count at the plate. Here's the pitch... Swing and a long drive into deep center field. Harrison is on the run. He dives... and makes the catch. Can you believe it, Kansas City? The Royals are World Champions. Harrison's career, forever defined by 'the Catch'."

John Harrison died from lung cancer four years ago, a year after Liam and Maggie moved to Nashville. A few months after his dad's funeral, Liam had an agent. Then a published novel. Then a major TV series. His father missed his son's success. Maybe it wouldn't have made a difference in their relationship; it didn't change things with his mother. The rejection drove him and crushed him at the same time—often at the expense of his relationship with Maggie. She was resilient through the mood swings and bouts of depression, just as he helped her deal with the insecurities imprinted from her childhood.

***

"Shake, pass out the script." Jack ordered Liam as a room of writers sat around an oak conference table. The room was messy and nondescript with bare, off-white walls that had been marked by the furniture that had been rearranged countless times. In one corner was an empty metal bookcase which housed, at its base, an unusually large collection of surge protectors. Outdated office furniture lined the opposite walls. Liam thought the furnishings looked like they had been inherited from a cheap hotel conference room. The kind of hotel stuck in the middle of nowhere in a room where the phrase, 'If these walls could talk' was never used. Liam snapped back and placed the story in front of each writer, and they began marking up the script. Liam felt alive. He couldn't believe he was at The Mill in London adapting his novel for a TV series. Jack could see the excitement on his face. He put his arm around Liam as if to say, you've arrived. Jack's affection made Liam uneasy. This is where Jack can be dangerous. It's like there's a mechanism installed in him that requires cruelty to offset the kindness. Not if but when he'd act. Liam didn't ask why, but how bad would it be. He needed to be alert but struggled from jet lag. He brought his mind back to the room to focus on the script.

The group emptied pots of coffee as they worked their way through what would be the pilot episode. Liam needed to balance openness with creative changes alongside his impulse not to let the story stray too far from its home. The novel is about betrayal. And Jack seemed intent on making that theme rhyme in real life. Even among close friends, the struggle for power lurks. Liam noticed Jack using 'I' instead of 'we' in the meeting. He manipulated the room like he's manipulated people his whole life. Due to the politics of the situation, Liam stayed quiet. He should be grateful for what Jack has done, right? Without Jack, there's no TV show. Jack is getting Liam's story in front of millions of people. Be grateful.

After work, they walked to the hotel. Jack discussed the plot.

"You think we have the right angle?"

"How do you mean?"

"I think we need to shine a light on the double-crossing wife. She's sympathetic to permanent revolution. But I don't want to spend a half-hour giving a history lesson."

"You don't think most people have an understanding of the Cold War?"

"No, I don't. Most people couldn't pass a basic civics class in their own country. I think assuming they understand the Cold War is a heavy lift. I'm not sure it matters, though, for the sake of our show. I think we zoom in on the personal side of the conflict. Intrigue. Betrayal. The audience doesn't need to know much about the broader conflict. What they can understand is deception and passion. We need to hit them with a message they can relate to—the universal truths. If we blow some shit up as we deliver the universal truths, we'll be golden. We can't be boring."

"I don't think we're boring. The audience can relate to the characters; see themselves in them. They recognize people like Peter Tufton or Rosa. But they should have a stake in the affairs of the world we're creating. I want them to feel like they are sitting in the middle of Europe in the 20th century. This isn't a documentary on the Cold War. We're telling a tale of deception. Yes, the betrayal of country, morals, and the betrayal of lovers. But is it betrayal when you think your cause is just? Tufton is our hero, but he's also an assassin. It's complicated. I think the messiness of things will keep people hooked."

"Hungry?" Jack said.

"Tired."

"You want to skip dinner?"

"I shouldn't."

"Good. This way."

They ducked into a quaint pub that was beginning to fill up with people mashing conversations into white noise. Jack dashed to the bar and ordered two pints. Liam found a booth and sat hard from exhaustion. He and Maggie shared a few text messages before Jack returned.

"I'm thinking of replacing the producer," Jack said.

"Already?"

"I'm not feeling the current situation. The producer's a pumpkin head."

"Maybe give him more than a day."

"I don't want to waste time."

"Do you have someone in mind?" Liam was nervous. This move seemed like Jack was playing for control.

"No, but I've already put out feelers. We need someone serious. This producer is a fountain of bad ideas; he'll ruin the show."

Jack was beaming with renewed swagger, and Liam marveled at his energy. He never seemed tired.

"We need more money. I've got this drug guy who's willing to help."

"Drug guy?"

"Legal drugs. Anyway, he's willing to put some cash into the project. He has ties to the government and can help remove any red tape we might encounter filming across borders. He says he's friendly with Gadly. I wonder if Maggie knows him."

"Is he trustworthy?"

"Doesn't matter. We need the money. He wants to be around the action. We'll tease him with Hollywood and keep him at arm's length. He's rich but harmless."

After dinner, Jack stuck around for drinks. He made friends with a group of locals and planned on making it a long night. Liam went back to the hotel to call Maggie. He told her what Jack said about the new investor. They came to realize this person must be George Davies, the former, and forever corrupt, vice mayor. She warned Liam to be careful with Davies. He said Jack had a team of people looking after them. Gadly thought he could handle Davies too.

The idea of George Davies investing in Liam's work made Maggie ill. Davies was like a spore. Adapting and surviving. Liam could get caught up in the corruption.

Jack was a man blinded by ambition and wasn't particular about who he associated with as long as they got him where he wanted to go. Maggie felt uneasy after hanging up on Liam. She busied herself with work for the rest of the afternoon to take her mind off Davies. In London, as his head hit the pillow, Liam slept like a dead man.

Maggie left the office and walked to a nearby coffee shop to work remotely. At a table in the corner, she paused scouring emails and watched for a minute as the barista prepared drinks. Ambient music played overhead, adding a layer of calm to the atmosphere. Maggie wasn't sure if it was Brian Eno, but it sounded like something from *Music for Airports*. Steam and milk. Some people studied; others ran small businesses. There was a table with four people. One did all the talking. The other three, staring at the one while she spit muffin and raised her voice to a thick drone like one of Eno's tape loops. One of those analog synths that sounds like a gull.

Maggie made plans for a company of her own. A PR firm but focused on work outside of politics. She wanted control. If she could control things, she could protect herself, and Liam.

She'd avoid men like George Davies. Gadly was smart but fell victim to the fear of failing. He lives in a higher class with disgust for the lower class. Disgusted because he knows he's only one circumstance away from being down... there. Gadly hoards success as a safety net from failure.

Pulling away from Gadly. A car reversing on a dark path. Like the night she found Caitlin in Gadly's office. Maggie had to be careful as she made her way down the hall. Don't make noise. Heel up, toe down. A quiet dance to the exit.

Maggie's freelance work wasn't enough yet to cover her bills, but she was getting closer. Liam's career was on the rise too. Though she was disgusted by Davies, she knew her time with Gadly was coming to an end. She'd focus on her work. Focus on assisting Gadly and try her best not to stress over the things she couldn't control.

After drinking another coffee, she sketched logos. All of them clean. As Maggie cycled through fronts, she forgot about George Davies and became lost in the promise of hope.

As she looked away from her laptop, she saw a print of John Coltrane's *Blue Train* hanging on the wall, near the bathroom. She studied his face. In the photo, Coltrane looks relaxed and curious.

Maggie needed a way to control the chaos around

her. Then she could relax. It was the through-line of her life.

7

A Gross Old Man

Gadly's work with Charlie Cheney is a cautionary tale of competing interests. One of Charlie's most skillful associates is George Davies, a virtuosic self-dealer. The story of his schemes is known. He's spent most of his working life cheating. He sniffs out where the line divides the rule of law and uses it to his advantage like a cudgel. He likes the sound of his own name. *Regulations won't tyrannize George Davies.* Soon he will infect everyone he's to encounter—including Maggie.

If irony is simulated ignorance, then what Gadly practices — willful blindness — is preservation. Self-preservation by being incurious to events happening right beneath his nose. Gadly, whose ethics loosen by the year, isn't interested in — to borrow a phrase — the means of production. Yes, Davies lives in a sea of racketeering, buoyed by slimy methods, but Gadly circles back to his natural state of convenient rationalizations—benevolent ends justifying dirty means. Realpolitik is his guiding light. Moralizers are bores who haven't seen the real world. Their idealism blinds them because the world isn't what they wish it to be. It is what it is, thought Gadly. Hackneyed and self-assured.

Caitlin, a woman of high character, oversaw the finances. If she wasn't raising a red flag, Gadly convinced himself, then everything would be fine. She had grown numb to Charlie's dealings — even keeping some of the money for herself — so she may not be the most reliable conscience here. With Caitlin's roots planted in a lavish lifestyle she couldn't — or wouldn't — live without, there wasn't a chance of walking away. There's something else in this, something more obvious. Gadly wasn't going to snoop around for the truth. He's not going to start the project of hunting for his demise. As noted earlier, Caitlin is good at her job. She knows Gadly well. She's studied his habits and memorized his insecurities. What she's come to learn is there isn't a line Gadly won't cross. Caitlin is pulling him across the Rubicon.

Dan was sent to Washington to meet with lobbyists. Dan, with Gadly's help, inserted himself on K Street— the nucleus of lobbyists and advocacy groups in the nation's capital. The 2018 midterm election season was in full swing. It's June and both cities — Nashville and DC — were hot. After decades of self-serving interests, America was now having to confront its first openly authoritarian party. Other parts of the world were asking a more direct question: Is democracy worth saving? The impulse for authoritarianism to deal with an impatient public gained traction in the West. That struggle can be localized with the assumed ascension of George Davies becoming Nashville's next mayor. On paper, Davies may not be as dangerous as someone with access to the nuclear codes but tolerated corruption at any level of power will chip away at the marble of democracy as any fine chisel will do. Sometimes the chisel is in the hands of an artist. But this chisel was wielded by the voters. One man isn't so scary until you realize he's a mirror looking back at the unserious people that put him in power in the first place. This conflict can be called many things. What it cannot be called is sustainable. George Davies cannot succeed without convincing good people to do bad things. Enter Dan Benchman, another ratchet in the box.

Dan went to Washington for one reason. Nashville is a health care city with a cash pool Davies and Gadly wanted to dip their toes into. Davies wanted the regulations to be loose. Part of Dan's mission was to make that message known. Dan convinced the Washington players that Davies was a reliable partner. A generous ally. His reach was deep not because he was the future mayor; his dealings in money laundering schemes had set up national politicians, and those cash avenues were propping up pliable members of Congress. The trick was to leave enough dirt on everyone's hands to assure mutual destruction should someone get the itch to snitch.

Upon his return, Dan was to meet Davies to discuss,

among other things, the upcoming election in August. They met at an upscale restaurant in the Gulch. Dan arrived early. He was staring at his phone while the combined noise of locals and tourists choked the air. You can distinguish tourists from the residents by the sound of their laugh. The cackle of a tourist will penetrate the atmosphere like a dull instrument. The streets fill with packs of out-of-towners laughing like lunatics as the vodka turns them into aimless jaywalkers who think the rules don't apply because they are on vacation. A gang of dufuses takes Dan's attention from his phone as they enter the restaurant with a ruckus. One of them — a grown man in a Marvin the Martian T-shirt — ruins the party as the manager turns him away. For a moment, Dan felt pity for him, then came to his senses when he imagined what dinner would be like sitting next to the rowdy visitors in cartoon shirts. Then Davies arrived and whisked the two away to a private booth inside.

Davies spoke with rapaciousness, pausing only to order a bottle of wine for the table. He told Dan he was investing in a TV series on a major streaming network. Davies was a repulsive figure missing most of the hair on top of his head, which contrasted with the abundance of fur growing down his nape like a garden of salt-and-pepper ornamental grass. He was red, swollen. Talking with a mouth full of dumplings and licking his fingers clean. Then he'd wash down his dinner with wine, making beastly noises resembling the orgasm of an octopus. Dan avoided the lobster shots and prayed gravity would keep his stomach where it belonged.

"Listen, Benchman. We are in the middle of something big here," he wheezed. "This is Hollywood. The timing couldn't be more perfect with the election just around the corner. My company is investing millions to produce this series. The press from this will erase what's been in the papers about my recent affairs. You see, as mayor, I'll work to lighten regulations on folks like me and good people like Gadly, who are trying to make this city great. We'll give them, *us*, the freedom to do business without the onerous threat of legalities getting in the way. We won the Cold War, goddammit. We won't stand for top-down, oppressive bureaucrats telling us how to do our business."

He continued. "That tyrant district attorney who came after me with bogus charges was just greasing the wheels for his next move. I know my way around Washington. I'll cut off his donor supply chain at the fucking knees. He thinks he has a shot at the vacant Senate seat. Ha. He'll finish his career alone in a hotel room in third place."

Davies was referencing the corruption charges he faced last year. It was front-page news at the time— something to do with no-bid government contracts. Charlie's name was implicated in the charges too. Davies convinced DA Jenkins to drop the charges by dangling donors to fund a run for the upcoming senatorial race. The donors agreed because they also needed to save face amidst the charges. They conspired with Davies to convince Jenkins he would be the next senator. Once they were clear of the implications, they planned to gut his campaign resources for retribution. He couldn't turn on Davies, because like a pro, Davies dirtied the DA's hands. He was finished. To turn up the heat, they ensnared Jenkins in a sex scandal. Stu Jenkins was a pious man who was part of the effort to make the Bible the official state book of Tennessee. Well, he was pious until he was found sending suggestive text messages to underage girls, and boys. Jenkins had no idea that the kids he was messing with were really Davies and his associates. Old God-fearing Stu Jenkins was now off the board thanks to some incriminating dick-selfies.

Dan forced a few bites of dim sum down his throat so he wouldn't give away his discomfort. He was tired of living under his father's thumb and thought George Davies was his best shot upward.

With Davies as his mentor, he felt like he was finally coming up for air. Yes, Davies was a gross old man, but Dan was attracted to the power. Not just the money but the power. Some people are repelled by men like George Davies and Charlie Cheney, but others attach to them like magnets. The opposing energies of ethics and corruption attract. Sausage is nasty, but tasty. Never mind it can kill you.

Davies kept talking. "If you want to play this game,

you gotta have sack, kid. You need skin as thick as a football. Look out for the press—those capricious little vultures. They'll do their best to back you into a corner. Put everything you say under a microscope. Remember this, Dan: never let them smell blood cause if it bleeds, it leads." The vulgarity was matched only by his insipidness.

Davies spoke in ridiculous terms. He used the language of a sewer rat. He was vulgar and functionally illiterate. He set aside no time for books but had a scholarly air when it came to matters of breaking the law. It was impressive to Dan. He watched as the man in front of him struggled to keep his chin clean from dinner. A raving psychopath who couldn't be bothered half the time to pull up his zipper. How could a man this meshuga move millions of dollars around the world? Dan was mesmerized by the puzzle. It was like watching a blind drunk who could only walk in a straight line if the line in front of him was a tightrope several stories high. Dan had no idea how he did it, but he was determined to learn the trade.

Dan spent the remainder of the dinner nodding along and doing his best not to vomit. After settling the bill, Davies mentioned an investment opportunity. He said they'd speak more about it in the coming days. Until then he needed Dan to be his eyes and ears inside Gadly's firm. Davies likes Gadly fine but saw young Dan as an impressionable ally, one who'd have his back regardless of changing circumstances. The meeting ended outside as Davies fetched a ride home. As the car waited, he reached for his phone; it must have buzzed inside his pocket. Dan whispered, "bye," leaving in the opposite direction to meet Michael for drinks—eager to tell him about the meeting. He was so dizzy with excitement that a cyclist nearly ran him over as he stepped into the bike lane without looking. Having avoided the crash, he smiled at Davies and went on his way. Waiting for Dan to be out of earshot, Davies answered his phone.

"Caitlin darling, how are you?"

8

Someone's Just Died

Maggie was stunned as she read the front page of the *Tennessean*. "Charles Cheney, Community Leader, Poisoned to Death."

"Who could have done this?" she said. Her heart broke for Caitlin. So much loss. Her daughter. Now Charlie, murdered.

Charlie Cheney's work had become so intertwined with Gadly; Maggie feared the killing might not stop with Charlie. Was Caitlin in danger? What about Gadly? Could her own life be at risk? She tried calling Liam, but his phone went straight to voicemail. She didn't leave a message.

According to the newspaper, Caitlin found him dead inside their home, face down on a hooked wool rug, arms and legs splayed, stuck swimming or commando crawling over a designer scene. It looked like he died while reaching for something, or someone.

When Charlie's body was turned over, his face was stuck in shock. Shock from the poison attacking his body or from a familiar face in the room. Hard to tell. There was a broken tumbler nearby. Scotch had spilled onto the floor. Toxicology reported the poison. Suicide ruled out. Caitlin insisted Charlie would never take his own life. No note. No evidence of a struggle. He might have been pacing in front of his desk. It was a nervous habit. Pacing and thinking. Thinking and pacing. Apart from adultery, pacing was Charlie's only exercise.

The news said nothing was missing. No forced entry. The killer must have been someone he knew. How else do you enter his home without disturbing anything? The report went on to say that Caitlin had arrived home that evening, finding Charlie dead in his study. His laptop was left open to emails, but nothing of consequence. The police took possession of the computer. Caitlin had been out with Gadly at a work-related meeting. Maggie wondered if the poison was planted ahead of time. Otherwise, the assailant seems to have vanished like a vulgar magic trick.

Maggie stood at her desk. Shocked. Eyes fixed on the headline when George Davies entered.

"Knock, knock."

"Um, hello," Maggie said. She focused on the news.

"I see you've heard the most unfortunate news about our dear friend, Charlie Cheney."

"It's hard to believe. Who would want him dead?"

"Let the authorities handle that, darling."

"Maggie," she said.

"Come again?"

"You can call me Maggie."

"Oh, don't be like that. You must know how Southern gentlemen are, so if you'd be kind enough to prepare the conference room for the meeting this afternoon. Gadly, young Dan Benchman, and I will be in attendance. Order enough food for the three of us. Sandwiches are fine."

Maggie always prepped the meetings. Gadly instructed her to take notes. At lunchtime, she'd set the table. Serve the food she'd ordered. There was never enough for her to eat. The first time this happened, she thought maybe she had been given the wrong headcount. She soon realized this was no mistake. What appeared to be a minor slight was indeed a larger message about her place within the company. Embarrassed as the team dined, she adapted by inventing busy work until it was time to clear the plates.

To her surprise, Caitlin entered the office. She didn't look like someone with a newly dead husband. Maggie marveled at her poise. Was this strength learned from losing Rebecca? She was strong. Always elegant. A skilled survivor. *Too skilled?* The idea that Caitlin might be her husband's killer rushed to Maggie's head. She felt guilty for suspecting her friend. A killer with sophisticated charm.

Quick, no more of this, she thought as she pushed the accusation away. She cherished Caitlin. Maggie tried to delete the impulse to place Caitlin in the room as the modish murderer. She couldn't help it. It wouldn't be the last time she thought Caitlin poisoned Charlie.

The killer had to be close. It didn't seem random. Nothing around here seemed random. Maggie envisioned the scene in the Cheney's fashionable home where Caitlin had grown to resent Charlie for turning cold after Rebecca's death. Dim lights. Expensive taste.

Charlie had affairs with women. He didn't go out of his way to hide them either. He flaunted these engagements, maybe as punishment, an effort to blame Caitlin for their baby's death. By his rationale, it was her body that failed—something she did wrong, causing Rebecca's heart to stop. Maggie continued with imagination; Charlie would show his wife what real power was. He'd have many women. There wasn't a damn thing she could do to stop it. But Caitlin is strong. Charlie underestimated his wife—a woman he seemed to know nothing about after years of neglect.

Caitlin needed a clean way out of this miserable marriage. She wanted to escape the loneliness of the house. It was a constant reminder of loss. Losing Rebecca was traumatic enough; she wasn't to blame. It was Charlie who failed. He failed when she needed him the most. She wouldn't stand by, humiliated while he lavished gifts on his new obsessions. So, she devised an old ploy to rid herself of him. She poisoned his drink. The plan was perfect. No one would dare accuse her of murder; there was already too much pity for her having lost a child. Caitlin is lovely, sad, vulnerable. Her husband, a greedy figure and womanizer, whose natural state is corruption, had it coming—fated by karma.

Maggie withdrew from her daydream. Snapping back to the office, she was surprised to see Caitlin walk in.

"I didn't expect you today. I'm so sorry about Charlie. Just awful."

"I won't be attending the meeting, dear. I need a quick word with Gadly then I'll be on my way." Caitlin didn't acknowledge Maggie's condolences.

"If there is anything I can do—"

Caitlin cut her off. "Please don't mention him. I can't bear his name."

As Caitlin left for Gadly's office, Maggie wondered whether, if Caitlin did have a hand in her husband's murder, she would come clean to Gadly. She might be overwhelmed by the desire to clear her conscience. The crime scene, according to the paper, was tidy. An inside job. Keeping something like this to herself would be impossible. A clearing of the chest would be her only way to redemption. Gadly would forgive her. He wouldn't let her go to prison. It was self-defense; he'd convince himself of this explanation. He'd have no choice because this is a matter of self-preservation, a matter of a passion they both share. Maggie did not want to go down this line of accusation, but the temptation was too hard not to indulge.

There must be another explanation. Caitlan didn't have it in her to be a killer. Maggie stopped herself, again, for the thought-crime against Caitlin. She couldn't have done it. Leave it to the detectives. Maggie had more in front of her anyway. The pressing matter was what to do with George Davies. His business with Gadly would bring more scrutiny under the lights of the upcoming election. The mayoral race converging with the death of Charlie Cheney was too much all at once. Her instinct was to run, but she couldn't. Not with Liam out of the country.

Gadly's business bloomed with Davies around. Apart from mourning his friend's death, Gadly was high on success. Regarding the company funds used for and by Davies, he didn't query too much about it. His infatuation with Caitlin provided a bulletproof distraction allowing Davies the freedom to act as chief operating officer. Maggie questioned the possibility or possible futility of decency among these people.

The work was fascinating. There was something about knowing what was happening in the city before it became news. Still, she remained conflicted. Maggie despised Davies. With his claws now locked in Liam's project, she saw no way out.

9

Catch the Stars

"When are you getting hitched?" Jack asked. Hard to hear over the crowded pub with half his attention on the football game on TV, behind Liam. They were in Hackney at one of Jack's preferred spots. It was noisy.

"Soon, I think. The timing never seems right. Maggie is slammed at work. My schedule with the show… I'm in another country. No need to rush, I guess. But I don't know. I want to marry her but there's always something in the way. Fuck."

"You won't find the perfect time. You should do it now. We'll look for a ring in London." Jack searched for little ways to find the kind of relationship propped up by Hollywood. It's what made him a great actor. His lines sounded like they weren't written. Like they just fell from his lips in the moment. Through circular logic, he'd make it true.

Liam couldn't wait to see Maggie again. She planned on joining them in London last week but got stuck in Nashville with work. Because of gaping time zones, they didn't talk every day. The times they did connect were interrupted by a loud pub or busy city street or Jack, shouting into the phone, stupid on whiskey.

The sound of Maggie's voice — a little raspy — melted Liam. While away, he daydreamed of her. Lips, matte red or natural—the upper lip peeking over the boundary of her mouth. There was a kindness to it.

She was clever. Liked history, Dostoevsky, and cars. She talked about Alyosha finding light in all that darkness in *The Brothers Karamazov*. Maggie used to tinker on car engines with her dad. Childhood wasn't all bad all the time.

Love is a distance. Maybe that's why it feels painful. Can feel painful. It's what separated Liam and Maggie. Love was the space between Liam and who he loved. That's how he thought about it.

There was something about being far away from her and the way desperation forced its way to the surface. Even with technology, the ocean that separated the two felt impenetrably large.

Random stories persisted. Maggie conflicted with her father. She'd also defend him to the death. Maggie and Alyosha's light. Little bits of randomness got rude and wrestled their way to Liam. She was far away but he could hear her voice retelling stories.

Her father wasn't always drunk or mean. He could be affecting.

Grease in the garage. Maggie liked the garage. The grease was evidence of something getting fixed. It's what fixed looked like in real time. She mimicked the way her dad held the wrench. Maggie's dad talked about torque. He'd tighten bolts with a wrench. That's static torque. Secure. But he'd also talk about torque as a force. The engine's crankshaft. Performance. Torque can be security and power. You need power to control things. If you can control things, you can have security.

The long-distance situation watered Maggie's self-doubt like a stubborn weed. With limited time to talk, precious minutes withered away fixing residual damage left behind from childhood. Liam sensed her tension as she waited for him to explode in rage as her father did. Those times in the garage when he couldn't fix the car. His frustration found Maggie like a guided missile.

The calls ended in therapy sessions and when they hung up, they felt the pang of having wasted the little time they had with the sound of each other's voices.

Liam told Maggie about the Italian actress playing Rosa. How they had connected on the set. She was perfect for this role. Beautiful. Seductive. Her large, brown eyes and the way her long auburn hair—

"Really," Maggie said.

"What?"

"Seriously? Are we at the part where you tell me about her perfect body?"

"I didn't mean it that way."

"In what way did you mean it then?"

He had nothing. Silence.

Maggie broke the pause. "My work is hell right

now. And you are in London talking to me about this girl. (Mimicking Liam): 'Beautiful. Seductive.'"

"I don't sound like that."

"That's not the fucking point, Liam. Have some self-awareness."

Liam was high from work. The excitement of being in London. It all clouded his decision-making. When they hung up, he'd be angry with Maggie. Was she jealous of his success? Maybe they shouldn't get married. He snapped out of this delusion and realized he messed up. The bitterness he aimed at Maggie was nothing more than an excuse. A deflection from his narcissism. He loved Maggie. Being apart was hard enough. Tomorrow will be better. He'll buy the engagement ring tomorrow.

The next morning, Jack blew off ring shopping which suited Liam fine. Liam wanted to shop for Maggie's ring without the distraction of Jack, over his shoulder, second-guessing each move. With Jack at a distance, they could speak freely on the phone. He apologized. She was in good spirits.

Ring shops have a way of making you feel like you've failed. Soft condescension from the salesperson pointing you to the ring cabinet in *your budget*. Yes, over here.

But he found it and celebrated the purchase by ducking in a nearby pub to escape the rain. The ring looked Victorian. Liam wasn't an expert but that's how he described it to Jack, on the phone.

Inside it was dark and warm. Low ceiling, dingy carpet, and cask ale. Liam found a small table near the fireplace. Downed a lukewarm pint and called Maggie. They spent the next hour talking. Laughing. This was the third time they had spoken today and each time he tried to find the nerve to propose. A third pint summoned the courage to do so. And all at once, as he started to ask, the call was interrupted. Maggie had to deal with work. Liam was relieved. Better to do it in person. He ordered another and reminisced on the story of how they met.

The details of Liam's years studying in New York aren't crucial to this story. What's important is that he returned to Kansas City after college.

High rent pushed Liam from the city. But he was fused to New York. He had to leave but it wouldn't leave him. He'd spend the next years of his life feeling pulled back to Manhattan. Not sure why. Probably just the same romantic nature of New York that lifted a poem from Walt Whitman. "Give me comrades and lovers by the thousand!" But living in New York was a little like hanging out with your best friend who's also a bully. New York reminded him of Jack. He thought about returning after paying off his school debt.

Back in Kansas City, Liam was hanging around his ex-girlfriend, Alex. She introduced Liam and Maggie and the three of them spent much of the summer together. Alex and Liam weren't dating again, but casually screwing. Liam used her to see Maggie. He wasn't aloof to the dangerous game he was playing. Liam flirted with Maggie as Alex looked on, peeved.

He was infatuated with Maggie, anxious with butterflies when she called. She wore a necklace that read: MEAT STINKS. It attracted his attention, and he imagined kissing her neck. She forgave him for eating animals, and he thought about giving it up. He teased he'd give up meat if she'd quit smoking. After several weeks of this, Alex needed to address Maggie about the situation.

"I don't mind Liam moving on, but I don't know that I can handle seeing him with my best friend."

"Do you think Liam is interested in me?" Maggie tried to bury her excitement.

"Are you serious? I see the way he looks at you. I see you stare back at him, you haughty bitch. I can't handle this."

"But you broke up before college. You've both dated other people. It's been over for years."

"If it's over then why did Liam fuck me last week?" Alex cried.

Liam has a history of impulsive decisions. A noticeable pattern. Prodigious at getting in his own way. Tempting fate by torpedoing what's good for him. When Maggie approached him with Alex's revelation, he wrestled his mind for a defense, saying they had only just met, and Alex convinced him Maggie was seeing someone else. Maggie let him squirm, enjoying his discomfort. She forgave him against her judgement, and they were inseparable over the summer. No more Alex. They'd hang out on Maggie's balcony until the sun came up, speaking about childhood, familial grievances, leaving Kansas City. They argued about music.

"You like that record?" He antagonized her about a Descendants album.

"I'll borrow one of your drippy albums when I want to be bored off my ass," she said. "What's up with Morrissey? To me, he's more Philip Larkin than Oscar Wilde. Don't you think?"

"Maybe. *Panic* is still great, though."

Liam didn't watch much TV, so Maggie filled in his pop-culture blanks. She talked about living in New Orleans. Then sneaking into shows to see bands when she'd go back to visit her cousins.

Maggie missed New Orleans but couldn't see herself living there again. Liam said they should go to New York, but she wasn't sure she could handle the density. Her mind changed after Liam surprised her with a trip to New York for her birthday. They saw a show on Broadway. Liam took her to St. Mark's Place, where they stayed for hours. She fell in love with the parks near East Village. The next day, he bought her a necklace at Chelsea Market. They talked about finding an apartment in the city, searched rentals online and became distracted by looking at places they couldn't afford.

Maggie introduced Liam to new foods. She loved

to dress him. She cut his hair. The first time they slept together, Maggie said, "Touch me all over." He drew her in by the waist. After sex, he'd trace the small of her back as she sat up and smoked — she had started again — while reciting Neil Young lyrics. He made her laugh. Maggie was there through his father's chemo treatments. She attended John's funeral.

Maggie felt safe with Liam. Liam put together the pieces of her ratcheted apart by the vicious words of her father. She felt confident with him. Theirs was a life shot on three cameras: the past, present, and future.

Liam was still in the pub, but his mind traveled back and forth over the years with Maggie. He was maudlin from the tepid pints and promised to protect her with his life. This made him laugh as he pictured Maggie asking if he was trying to use one of Jack's lines on her. Liam knew how earnest it sounded but something made him say it anyway.

Buying the engagement ring was supposed to be about the future. But Maggie was struggling back home. Charlie's murder clouded everything. All of this came into focus with George Davies. Did Jack know what he was doing, working with Davies? Liam could feel his life was now speeding and he was losing control of the wheel.

10

Struggle for Power

Maggie couldn't sleep thinking of George Davies investing in Liam's TV show. She hated being a part of anything to do with him, yet at the same time she recognized Liam's opportunity. George Davies and Charlie Cheney had been crooks for years. The mayor threatened to act against them. They retaliated by forcing Mayor Binks to resign after they dug up an old scandal. It came out in the news that he had fathered a child with his wife's identical twin. This was years before he held office. His daughter, Charlotte, learned that her aunt was her biological mother after seeing it trending on social media. The poor girl was away at college at the time. The bloodless intrusion into her life forced her to drop out of school, exiled from peers. Her friends tried to be encouraging, but they were not the ones on the receiving end of an online mob, feeding on her privacy like starved lions. The mayor had a high approval rating. He tried using his popularity to offset *Twingate*. The avalanche of press chipped away at the goodwill he'd banked. Once the national reporters arrived, the pressure became too much. The city's power structure wasn't going to trade 'it' status to save a kinky mayor. He had to go. The episode called for a special election, thus opening the door for George Davies. This wasn't three-dimensional chess. Cheney and Davies created their luck by staying in the game. Put another way, they survived. They sustained a war of attrition among the grifters. Arriving at a pot of gold at the end of a crooked rainbow.

The Binks affair was a gift, creating a power vacuum for Davies to fill. There was no stopping him now. Charlie was the mastermind. Davies, the face. Neither of them knew shame. The reality is you can't shame the shameless which means there isn't a depth with which they wouldn't reach. The rule of law relies on an honor system. Checks and balances become impotent when the people in power are no longer doing the checking. Or balancing. Tyranny today won't look anything like the bloody struggles of the 20th century. People will continue to go about their day; working, buying groceries, taking kids to school. What happens instead is that self-dealing politicos embed themselves in power like ticks. Maybe politico isn't the correct word here. Some of these people are ideologically rigid, but others are opportunists with a nose for the zeitgeist. Once in power, the rules will change, and it becomes impossible to remove them. The Constitution has holes. Find them. Use them. It's not illegal.

Sympathetic pundits act like state TV, flooding their viewers with disinformation. In addition, social media provides the perfect tool for bullshit to spread like an uncontrollable cancer. Distracted voters fight with neighbors and family members over trumped up culture wars while men like George Davies and Charlie Cheney rob the state to enrich themselves. To make things worse, a reactionary press turns journalism into activism because it thinks it's holding power accountable. But it's stuck in a desperate gambit for subscription dollars to survive the digital storm. Radicalized. Counter-radicalized. Little by little, the mechanisms for accountability fail. Truth is subjective as people select narratives like they're picking fruit at the market.

Everything about Davies stank. Now his dirty money was being used to finance Liam and Jack's show. The sham pharmaceutical manufacturing company was swelling with cash. They needed to clean the money. Davies and the company got creative by funding network TV using dummy shareholders to hide the fraud. He had people positioned in banks where he could move the money unnoticed. A young writer with his friend — an actor transitioning to director — were too ambitious, too naïve to see the schemes. The perfect marks. The same move was copied and passed across industries. Once the money began flooding political campaigns, there was no way to shut it down because the people in charge of writing the laws were put there by this money. Each time Davies left a meeting after closing another deal he'd say, "Squeaky clean."

Charlie swept the trail, but now he's dead. Davies is greedy, but he needs someone like Charlie to cover his tracks. The old boy was too sloppy to handle it alone. Maggie's admiration for Caitlin kept suspicion at bay. She was desperate to speak with Gadly alone. He has no clue what he's in the middle of, but he trusts Maggie. She needed him to know how dire things had become. She wanted him out of his stupor. Shake him loose from the allure of Davies. Maggie needed to press the issue but didn't know how. With the murder of Charlie Cheney, she now feared for her life.

Davies knew Maggie could be a problem, though sensing her fear, he thought he could keep her under control by staying close. Make her feel good about the work they were doing. Busy her with important tasks. Davies welcomed Maggie's ideas. He swooned over her proposals — even the pedestrian ones — at meetings. He once sent her to lead a civil rights breakfast knowing how much she admired the local leaders heading the initiatives. Davies waited for the moment when Maggie felt the rush of a project launching her from assistant to account manager, moving past the self-imposed limitations of being a college dropout. To the place where her father would finally approve.

Then the harassment began. Davies dehumanized her with innuendo. His empty mentoring neutralized the inappropriate comments about her body. He talked about her shoes. He sank further: "Where do you work out?" Or: "I wish my wife dressed like you."

She, in turn, played it off as the outdated actions of a man from another generation. But Davies never let up. "I bet you're fierce in bed." Then the pervert played it off in jest.

"If you have questions about the spreadsheet, let me know," Maggie responded. She changed the subject, wanting to crawl out of her skin.

Davies hung out in Maggie's office when he didn't need to be in the room. He greeted her with a hug and a hand on her lower back. One afternoon in the narrow kitchen, as she put away the office groceries, he walked by and slid his hand up the back of her leg across the line of her underwear. A ruse that he was only passing by in a tight space. Maggie couldn't plead her case to Gadly because his business now hinged on the new relationship with Davies. Maggie's promotion would never come. She was disposable.

Life is a struggle for power, and Maggie felt powerless. When you experience these things over and over, the will to push back begins to atrophy. Power flows downhill. She was suffocating from humiliation. From professional disappointment. Maggie placed her ambitions aside; she didn't want to be the one to blow Liam's opportunity. This burden added to her struggle. She had so many questions about her future, but the one most pressing was this: What is Liam's fate?

Maggie couldn't put off telling Liam about the situation at work with Davies, but they'd had trouble connecting. She needed to alert him without Jack standing there. A text wouldn't do because Jack might see the notification. She planned to tell Liam in person when he arrived home from London. He was due back in a few days. In the meantime, she'd do her best to handle Davies.

Back in London, Liam was growing frustrated with Jack. He felt pushed out by so much, having changed from the book to the script. Jack wasn't dedicated to the story as much as he was to success. His success. The more he controlled, the more he removed his friend. Liam had become a bystander. When they began the partnership, Jack assured Liam creative control. The situation changed with George Davies. The money he brought in lifted the series to a new level with a budget to film internationally instead of duplicating cities on a soundstage. Jack wanted the series to look like a major motion picture. Davies convinced Jack to take control.

Liam did get caught up in the excitement with the rest of the team. They went out for drinks to celebrate their new producer. Her name is Abam, a Nigerian now splitting time between New York and London. Abam is a critic's darling who swept the award season last year with her documentary, *New Terrorism*, on the rise of political extremism in America. She brought a seriousness to the project, rescuing it from the cheap drama it was heading for under Jack's direction. Abam checked Jack's instinct to overindulge. Liam was relieved to have her around.

To complicate matters, Jack and Abam had fallen

in love. The two were inseparable. As the flirtations carried on, fewer people were allowed in the decision-making. Liam was happy for Jack to find love but was angry at being cut out. It brought back the memories of betrayal from high school. Though a decade has passed since graduation, some wounds still hurt. Back then he stood looking through the window while Jack held his girlfriend. Now he stands again on the outside as Jack co-ops his book. Liam saw Jack acting in reverse voyeurism—gaining pleasure watching him watch Jack take what he wants.

11

A Meeting is Required

Maggie met Dan and Gadly for lunch at a buzzing joint in Dan's neighborhood. It was midday, and Dan had requested they meet in East Nashville because he was having work done at his house and needed to remain nearby on the chance, he'd have to *get in someone's face*. A massive renovation with a photo studio for Michael was growing out of control like a live organism working its way through Dan's bank account. Dan was pale with stress, which only added to the ongoing tensions with Michael. Intimacy was gone. They had devolved from partners to roommates. The house, now torn apart, revealed a darkness; fresh paint and décor hid structural issues. Dan and Michael seemed close to others, but cracks were beginning to appear with the mounting stress in their lives.

Gadly began the meeting by raising glasses in memory of his friend, Charlie Cheney. He reflected on their childhood: fishing, one-on-one basketball games in the park, chasing girls. He spoke with satisfaction of the success they enjoyed. The success of Nashville.

It was Charlie's idea for Gadly to open the firm. At the time, Gadly was providing legal counsel for state officials. He was bored of the work. He watched Charlie get rich in the drug market. Gadly wanted some for himself.

Charlie confided in Gadly about Caitlin. He loved his wife, but after losing Rebecca, the couple grew apart. They stopped speaking to each other, living in separate wings of the house. He hadn't shared a bed with Caitlin in years; the sex stopped even earlier. Gadly's wife was alive at the time, but they never had kids. Gadly didn't want them. After Rebecca died, he tried consoling Charlie, awkwardly explaining how difficult it was when he and Marie lost their cat, Sponges. Charlie traveled a lot for work, and it stressed the marriage. While traveling, he'd only cheated on Caitlin four times, or maybe five times—he lost track of count. They were meaningless flings. He did remember Cynthia, a stewardess he met on a flight for business in Scandinavia. They vacationed in Morocco in Casablanca—he fell in love with her there. He had never been to North Africa and was basking in newness. He took her dancing. When Charlie grew tired of dancing, he'd escape to the bar, to order Johnnie Walker Black, to watch her dance. Cynthia moved with elegance. He loved the way she smiled, a mischievous smile as her hair fell across her nose. Cynthia's magnificence made you think Photoshop worked outside the computer. Her long legs looked like Bernini sculpted them at his peak.

Charlie showered Cynthia with gifts. Only George Davies knew of the affair. He had set up a bank account for Charlie to fund the affair outside Caitlin's notice. Charlie then hired Cynthia as an additional executive assistant; one did the work while his lover had an excuse to be on his constant travel.

Though Charlie acted with deception, he justified his actions by his feelings for Cynthia. This isn't a fling, he'd say. In the same way he explained his crimes by how much the city was improving. When he referred to *his* city, he meant it. Charlie and Davies commended themselves on rebuilding blighted neighborhoods or designing a new development on the Cumberland; these victories were worth the price taxpayers had to pay for progress. Does that legitimize the crimes? Crime is subjective because laws can change. An offense under the current law is only part of the process of buying time until removing the odious barrier. The Cheney's grew apart. He tried fixing his marriage, but he couldn't any more than the doctors couldn't resuscitate Rebecca. Instead, he fixed himself up neat, and the city he loved.

Gadly spoke to his friend. "Charlie can't be blamed for a cruel world."

Gadly continued by reciting something Charlie said, "You can't let pain take root and ruin you. Return serves and uses cruelty as a survival tool. When Rebecca died, Caitlin's light went out, and my love was no longer welcomed. She's warm to everyone around her except me. Though she didn't blame me, she did see me as a reminder of the most tragic loss a mother could suffer. I was shown a black flag, sent to the pits, rooted in her mind, marking the futility of God. How could God allow a newborn baby to die? Did God choose not to save Rebecca? Then He's wicked. Could He not save Rebecca? Then God is impotent.

"In the hospital, I was on my knees, pleading with the sky. Like a fool, I sobbed. Begging for a savior who remained silent. Caitlin wept from her bed with a sound so stricken with agony, amplified by the vision of my baby girl — blue and lifeless — desperate for oxygen. I was lost, blubbering like a child trying to save my child through incantations. Caitlin may not blame me on my face, but she hates me. I don't blame her. I do love Caitlin, but I, too, need to be loved. Rebecca would have loved me, but she's gone. I would have been… Dad. I would have kissed Rebecca's head. Fixed her sadness. Rebecca would have reached for me, learning to walk. Maybe 'Daddy' would have been her first word. She'd have grown into an exquisite woman, like her mother. Like Caitlin, Rebecca would have been kind and smart, and she'd be the rainbow this gray world needed. I'll never get the chance to scare off her boyfriend, see her off to college or walk her down the aisle. This unspeakable loss is my fate. Pardon me if I want to dance with Cynthia. In these fleeting moments, I feel alive. I take in the air of affection, knowing when it's over, I'll return to the water, unable to breathe again."

Gadly returned the conversation to Dan and Maggie and how they'd move forward with the company. Maggie, concerned, wondered who might have wanted Charlie dead. Dan interjected that anyone could have killed him. Charlie worked in *legal drugs*, a loathed industry, whose enemies are countless. The killer using poison was symbolic of the drugs Charlie was selling. He got rich pushing drugs for prescriptions. In return, he swallowed a lethal cocktail. Gadly nodded with approval. Maggie was curious that nothing had gone missing as if the sole intention was removing Charlie. He was found dead inside his home. Nothing else was disturbed. Charlie kept stashes of money in places throughout the house. Caitlin told Maggie that she found stacks of large bills in various drawers. On occasion, Caitlin grabbed a little for herself. For shopping. She hid away a cash pile in the event Charlie ever left her. He never questioned the missing cash. Curious, Charlie's killer took the life of a well-known wealthy man but didn't bother pinching anything from the house. The goal was to erase Charlie Cheney. But why?

Gadly said Caitlin had been coming to him for consolation. He wanted to highlight a particular conversation he found important to share. Before Charlie's poisoning, Caitlin and Gadly met for dinner.

After eating, they stayed for hours in a booth, talking, drinking. She talked about Rebecca and the unfortunate state of her marriage, about love and loss. As the waiter refilled their glasses, Caitlin mentioned a lover.

"Charlie and I never healed after Rebecca died. I don't think either one of us had the want for the strength to try. Charlie was married to his work. He had other lovers and was always a bad liar. I heard him, in the late hours, whispering into his phone. I didn't resent him for it. I knew the pain was unbearable. If these flings bandaged his heart, I cared enough for him to let him have his joy. I don't seek pity, but my pain is different. Rebecca grew in my body, and I failed. My body failed Rebecca. I failed Rebecca. For that, I cannot forgive myself.

"Charlie cursed God. He chose to live under a dome of darkness. I still find beauty in the ideal of God. I see poetry in nature. The verses are God—freed from religion. God is the name we give to things we don't or can't understand. God hides within us. *She* — men don't own the numinous — can be the answer for what we can't explain. I'm content with that. Rebecca is my God. I won't curse Her. Charlie is a nihilist who refuses to listen to another song. He's too cynical for poetry. I needed light after losing my daughter. I couldn't allow Charlie to extinguish it forever. My husband is a powerful man, but I won't give him that power. I wanted nothing more to do with him. It's terrible to say, but the sound of Charlie's voice filled me with contempt.

"His infidelity made it easier on me. My work gave me focus; otherwise, I might never have left the bed. I needed to laugh. Yes, I smiled often, but years passed without laughter. My smile was nothing more than a bow on top of an empty gift. I felt like the big house I lived in — ornate, warm on the outside — was cold and empty within. Charlie's traveling made the house feel wintry. Vacant. I had to fill that void. I wanted to laugh again."

Caitlin paused. Gadly took her hand. She brushed aside a blonde wave of hair as she smiled. Doing her best to keep back tears. Gadly wondered why we have the impulse to cry at times of happiness. He guessed it was a balancing act of nature. He was sharing a piece of Caitlin's storm; his loss — his deceased wife, Marie — balanced Caitlin's. With Gadly, she laughed again. He didn't feel guilty for having feelings for his friend's wife. Charlie had given him the justifications on a silver platter. They bonded in a shared tragedy. Intoxicated by the possibility of leaving behind anguish.

That evening, they found their way to Gadly's office down the street. That's how Maggie came to see them on his couch. As Caitlin removed her blouse, she let loose the ghost inside. When they touched, they switched between tenderness and Darwin—something forbidden making the affair too tempting to avoid.

In his hands, she became an object. Gadly pulled her hair as he kissed her neck. Then he was in her hands. Caitlin forced her way on top of him with a smile. Every emotion, every tension was released. When Caitlin wrapped her legs around Gadly, it wasn't just sexual. She clung to him. Holding on. Hope. Now they are together.

Affair suggests conflict. Entanglement. The question of morality focuses on immorality. Caitlin and Gadly were running toward each other. They needed each other. Their lives were chaos and conflict. The affair had the potential for more conflict. Unspoken in the sex was the opening for a solution. A doorway was the way out.

A thing most vivid to Maggie's recollection was the sound of Caitlin's laughter. It was unrecognizable to her. Maggie hadn't seen Gadly this happy either. How could something so shocking still have a tinge of beauty to it? She thought the affair was a scandal at the time, but the real scandal was barreling down on them with Charlie Cheney's poisoning. His murder unleashed a series of events touching them all, including Liam.

Maggie was upset about Liam's show being tied up with Davies, but Gadly brushed it aside. Davies poured money into all kinds of things. What they needed Maggie to focus on was the upcoming election. Maggie shook her head with acknowledgment but felt something sinister was afoot.

12

Parallels in a Pod

Maggie was giddy for Liam's return. He'd been away in London for three weeks—the longest they'd ever been apart. Frayed by the stress, by the excitement of meeting Liam at the airport, she spent the afternoon emptying her closet for the right thing to wear. Maggie applied lipstick, tussled with her hair, stood in front of a full-length mirror—turning to look at her backside. Feeling ready, she grabbed her purse, the keys from the kitchen counter, down the stairs through the door in a hurry. In the car, she struggled with how to tell Liam about Davies harassing her at work.

Maggie spent a good deal of work-life navigating the troubled waters of abuse and harassment. Do the job. Dodge the creeps. Don't be a bitch. Part of the day is an exercise in balancing emotional mind-fucks — such as men invading your personal space or wondering whether this monster is too essential to report — with the work itself.

Liam was standing outside baggage claim. She was a few cars back in a snail-like procession. Liam waved, headed her way, dragging his luggage. Maggie could see a busted zipper on his suitcase. This made her laugh as she pictured Liam packing the morning for his flight. Shoving the clothes inside with a knee on the suitcase, ruining the zipper in the process. She guided her car to the curb, got out and waited. Liam arrived and they held tight to each other, ignoring the airport security, moving them along.

On the ride home, they caught up on the lives they lived apart. Liam talked about London. About the show's progress. Maggie talked about a plumbing nightmare at the apartment. Now fixed. In London, it sounded like Liam and Jack had visited every pub, doing their best to drain the city's cask beer. Liam said he had the best curry in England.

On a weekend trip to Manchester, Liam and Jack worked their way through Rusholme; Liam ordered korma, mild; Jack ordered vindaloo, hot. Jack felt the need to impress, as he does, telling the waiter, after being warned, he could handle the heat. As dinner wore on, Liam could see Jack beginning to sweat.

The vinegar and spices made his attempts at cool futile; hot face and watery eyes won the tug-of-war. No amount of water would check the mouth volcano that was now in full control of Jack's body. Liam suggested milk but Jack refused, insisting on water. To make matters worse, they were both drunk on Kingfisher. Jack — sloppy and smoldering — could barely handle his wallet.

Back at the hotel, Jack was in the bathroom pissing out hot spices as he begged for it to end. The ridiculous episode ended with Jack passing out in his clothes, lying in bed like a beached Hades, jetlagged from the underworld.

All this talk of food made Liam hungry, so they stopped for a late lunch, near the apartment. At the restaurant they discussed Davies and the show. Maggie went through a long list of his shady business dealings, warning Liam to be careful. Liam said Jack mentioned Davies, almost in passing. Jack wasn't stressed about his involvement. Davies was a snake among snakes in the TV business. Liam's attention was on the script. Jack's indifference fed Maggie's anxiety.

Liam was concerned about the situation in London. It had nothing to do with George Davies. Jack had fallen in love with Abam, the new producer. Together, they had shrunk the creative team. Jack now controlled the script. Within the micro-tyranny, Abam was in charge.

Liam admired Abam. The show was in good hands. But he felt betrayed by Jack once again. Maggie was livid. She knew how easily Jack could hurt Liam. She watched this play repeat itself over and over. Jack's betrayal became life imitating art like Rosa double-crossing Peter Tufton in Liam's spy novel. Maggie saw another parallel as she noticed her own similarities with Caitlin.

Caitlin left college early and survived a cold, unhealthy marriage. Maggie, too, had quit school and survived the verbal attacks of her father. As mentioned earlier, they shared a love of vintage fashion and vintage cars, French film, and red wine. Maggie saw in Caitlin an old soul like she was staring at herself in a rear-view mirror. They fixed up their lives secretly, suffocating pain beneath what was visible to the outside world. It was like climbing a mountain for Caitlin to move past Charlie, to find laughter again, to find love. To love. Finally, Maggie, stopped seeking approval from a father who wouldn't bend. As difficult as that was, it wasn't the most challenging part. She had to reverse the hatred and cynicism. Stop the cycle. Caitlin did the same. She sought the light Charlie had extinguished. When her husband settled on nihilism, she found faith. Caitlin cherished her pregnancy while Charlie focused on the time unlived—the time lost. To Charlie's thinking, where he stops stands in the way of what's missing— like a sound wave dispersing molecules. Caitlin saw Rebecca as forever a part of nature. Once born, a body may die, but the spirit lives on. Her memory is her spirit. Rebecca effectuated Caitlin like an echo pinging the universe with the call and response of life. Living and dying, laughing, weeping. Space. Time.

Maggie also saw an analog between childhood friends: Charlie and Gadly; Liam and Jack. Envy and competitiveness between friends are nothing new, but Charlie's poisoning wouldn't leave Maggie's attention. Gadly and Caitlin's recent love affair, predating the murder, added intrigue. Caitlin had what she wanted, so the thought of her killing Charlie didn't fit the sinister reality.

Charlie made Gadly. The firm wouldn't exist without Charlie or his connections. Then he unwittingly gave Gadly an apogee, Caitlin. Through bitter liaisons, Charlie made a future for Gadly in Caitlin's exquisite scent, sublime intellect, beauty. He gave his friend the one thing Caitlin kept—her laughter. Laughter is more than the sound of mirth; it's the sound of comfort. Safe resignation. Charlie didn't care to see it at the time because he busied himself with licentious recovery from the unending pain of losing his daughter.

Since he could no longer be a father, he'd carry on as a libertine. Travel the world and take and take and take. Charlie gorged on a buffet of women and money. Craving power like a trapped dog leaving the basement, finally exposed to fresh air, daylight, raw meat. Having already experienced a devastating loss, Charlie vowed never to lose again. His madness concealed the truth that he had already reached a zero point. As he raked, snarled, and barked his way through existence, he missed one essential fact: There was going to be another loss. Make those two more losses. First, Caitlin; then another he would assist as he raised a glass laced with poison to his lips—his life.

As Maggie pondered the other side of the friend set, she recalled Jack kissing Liam's girlfriend in high school. Not the same but coupled. It's a story Liam retold to Maggie. With each rerun, she saw his pain. Maggie thought Liam might have missed what to her seemed apparent: the possibility that Jack knew Liam would come upon the scene. Jack invited Liam over as he arranged a date with Caroline. The curtains were drawn open, so anyone could see what was happening in the bedroom down below. Oblivious to what he was to witness, Liam crouched to knock on the window. Inside he saw Caroline in Jack's arms, laughing— laughing as Caitlin would many years later with Gadly. Though most thought Jack had it all, what he didn't have was Caroline. Maggie didn't ask Liam about this possibility. She was afraid it would ruin him. So, she kept it, like the other pain burdens she held inside to protect the ones she loved. Maggie never confronted her parents. She absorbed the abuse, survived it, and moved on. She had a way of tossing trauma like pennies to the back of her mind. But pennies add up after a while; at some point, the fountain runs out of room. It overflows. Maggie could feel the water rising. She was hoping Liam wouldn't drown in it too.

13

Three Worlds

Abam arrived in America to study at NYU. She's now lived on three continents. The difficulties of balancing these different worlds are a central part of her story. At school, it didn't take her long to feel 'American.' She made friends and fell in love with the culture. Enamored by Broadway, she'd landed in the United States to be a storyteller. Part of her journey, part of what made the balancing act so tricky, were the frequent reminders of her otherness. Outside her circle of friends, strangers saw her as 'foreign.'

She wondered, What is America? Is it a place for immigrants? Are immigrants welcome only in certain parts of the country? From certain countries?

Abam became a citizen, though even with citizenship, she felt like an outsider. America has a unique sense of self-superiority. Its politicians are obsessed with American greatness. What exactly does that mean? In American life, she noticed a lack of interest in other cultures beyond exterior things like food or fashion. Maybe it has to do with America being protected by oceans. It's much harder to travel to other countries and experience different cultures than it is in other parts of the world. But Abam *did* think America was great. In America, she was able to achieve something that wasn't possible in Nigeria. But without Nigeria, she wouldn't be who she is. The longer she lived in New York, the more American she felt.

Growing up in Nigeria, in Zamfara, Abam spoke Hausa and English. Linguistically, there was always a balancing act. Like many expats, Abam struggled with what to keep and what to discard. Throwing away boxes of stuff is one thing. It's harder to let go of pieces of culture. Think of a young adult changing the religion they were brought up in. Or losing their religion. College, for most people, is a place of exposure. It's a space to challenge a pre-existing worldview. A widening of the lens. Abam welcomed the new experience, but she did struggle. After several years in New York, she moved to London. Three continents. Two languages. One woman even a flood couldn't stop, explained later.

In their hotel room, Jack listened as Abam suggested they change the show's title to *The Twin Affair*. Jack agreed as he studied the smooth dark skin that hugged her defined cheekbones. They faced each other in bed as Abam repeated the stories she thought up as a little girl in Africa, with dreams of one day sharing those stories on the big screen.

Jack's narcissism diminished around Abam. He

gave himself to her. Abam cured Jack of selfishness, most of the time. She freed him from resentment and encouraged him to find space for Liam. Jack was intimidated by Liam's wit. Abam urged Jack to cherish his friend's mind. Be open.

"Art is impossible if you're not willing to get out of the way." Abam said. "Your work isn't about you. Too much *you* and the work will crumble under the weight of insecurity."

He acquiesced. Abam had wisdom from a worldly life. Her childhood was conflict. A struggle he didn't know. Still, she survived.

"Baby," she said. A maternal sobriquet even though he was three years older. "Do you believe there is no more to your life than the events of your experience? Live outside yourself like the spaces between the lines. When you read a book, your imagination fills the gaps. Always leave space; otherwise, the story will suffocate. Stories need to breathe like we do. When you feel lonely, that could be the space your story needs." She pressed her fingers against her cheek. Abam continued. "You cannot take back how you've hurt your friends any more than you can't catch up on missed sleep.

"You can be the shadow, the light, the surface. But if you choose only one, you'll be stuck like a shadow— a dark, threatening companion that is both something and nothing at the same time. A surface alone can be hard. Cold. Light is nourishing, but you can't hold or harbor anything with it. You are guarded. We all are.

Stop using your hands to push. Reach out. Quit forcing your way along the old roads. We need bridges. Build a fucking bridge, baby."

Abam laughed. She sat up in bed, grabbed nail polish from the side table, and began painting aqua onto her toenails.

Taking Abam's advice, Jack phoned Liam. They picked up where they'd left off. They were eager to finish the final edits, discussing Peter Tufton's twin brother from the novel.

Phillip and Peter were separated at birth. Their father died young, leaving their mother without the means to raise the children. They grew up in orphanages fifty kilometers apart, outside of London. Maturing into young boys, they became aware of each other but didn't find a way to meet until adulthood. The brothers were close but led separate lives. Peter, an adventurer, joined British intelligence, while Phillip lived what most considered a normal life. He married a Russian woman named Feodora. They raised two daughters in a small cottage in Hull. Phillip drove a truck — a lorry in England — and supplemented his income with odd manual labor jobs. According to rumor, Feodora's mother knew Trotsky. She had worked for him, delivering his letters clandestinely while living near Fontainebleau. That was 1934. Trotsky landed in Mexico in January 1937. Feodora was born in '35.

Feodora was a believer and would debate with

Peter during his visits. Peter argued that Trotsky would have been as evil as Stalin because he would have done anything to keep power. She shot back that Stalin perverted the Revolution. She, too, hated Brezhnev and how he awarded himself medals. Peter answered that Trotsky only wrapped his viciousness in great oratory. Then he went after Lenin, proclaiming that his hagiography was due to his having died too soon. Feodora countered using Trotsky's argument that revolution is the impossibility of changing society by reason. She said revolution can be planned but it cannot be planned out. How can violence be averted when you are up against conflicts of interest, money fetish, and exploitation? She despised the British government, but her anger kept her from seeing the great freedom she had to do so.

Phillip wasn't interested in politics, but he did seek adventure. So, when Peter recruited him on a mission, he jumped at the chance. Phillip had never met Rosa; he was only familiar with some photographs. She was beautiful. He couldn't imagine by looking at her in the photo how dangerous she had become. They went over the plan and then rehearsed it again and again. Peter warned his brother not to be seduced by Rosa. If Phillip gave in to her ways, the mission would fail, and they'd wind up dead. If the plan failed, the last thing they'd see would be a farewell kiss, blown like a slow feather, sealing their fate.

Feodora knew nothing about this scheme. Peter was

sure he couldn't trust her — not because she was compromised — because she might say too much when visiting friends in town. If a mole had reached the highest levels of power, you could assume others were hiding among the commoners.

Jack and Liam were satisfied with the story. Abam approved. She delighted in their renewed friendship. Over time, Maggie and Abam grew close, which eased her concern about Jack. Abam was good for Jack. A kinder Jack was good for the world—especially Liam and Maggie's.

14

Curious Mayor Binks

"How could this happen?" Mayor Binks was enraged. "Who cares what I've done in my personal life? My administration has accomplished great things for this city. People think George Davies has character. Just you wait. Public office will become his personal business. The two will be one."

The mayor said, "They've ruined me. They ruined my career. My marriage. My daughter's life. Those sons-a-bitches."

Binks couldn't hide his contempt for Davies while his chief of staff, Reg, looked on in silence, knowing it was best not to speak. He was there only as an intake machine for his boss's anger. Reg was an ally. One of the remaining few who didn't quit the mayor after the scandal.

"Davies deserves the same fate as Charlie Cheney. The two of them orchestrated my takedown." The disgraced mayor paced his study. He held a large pen in his right hand, shaking it to emphasize points of rage. He aimed at Gadly next. He felt betrayed by his friend.

Binks and Gadly worked together to make Nashville what it is today. Gadly helped Binks become mayor. Now Gadly ignores his calls.

"Who does he think he is?" Binks said. "He stabbed me in the back. He double-crossed Charlie—sleeping with his dead friend's wife." The mayor was spitting, raising his blood pressure. "I see what's going on here. If they think I'll go away quietly, they are mistaken. I'll bury those criminals. I'll bury them all."

Reg intervened. "Sir, we need a plan. They can't get away with this. Davies can't be allowed to win the upcoming election. He must be dealt with."

"How do you mean?"

"I see an opening. But the window will be closed soon. We must act with expediency."

Binks was wild. "You are speaking in math. Come clean with your proposition."

"Charlie's poisoning is a mystery. While there is a cloud of suspicion hanging over the case, we can take advantage by striking Davies with chaos in the air. Think of this, George Davies, who by the nature of his business dealings, mingles with criminals. Suppose we create a situation where we choke off the income streams of his most dangerous benefactors by killing his supply chains. We can set it up in a way to make it look like Davies pocketed the money. Their money. We'd use their hand as our own to strike him down. When he draws his final breath, we'll make it known to him who held the knife."

"Do you have access to the type of people who can handle this for us?"

"Yes, sir. I know just the men."

"They would have to be... discreet. It can't be messy."

"The scene will be tidy, sir." Reg was pleased with himself.

Binks moved into a mode of justifying the bloody crimes they were planning.

"Some laws get in the way of dealing with scoundrels. Here, nature's laws are better suited. You see, Reg, a man must have the courage to break the law in matters of righting a wrong. The sum of a man's actions shall seal his fate. We are only acting as instruments to bring about a resolution to this matter. George Davies guaranteed his demise by ruining a wonderful family. My family. My daughter did him no wrong. Though I have rendezvoused on several occasions with my wife's twin, it was a private affair between consenting adults. My wife had been left in the dark for her protection. Her sister, spitefully, broke the news that devastated my wife. It took great effort to save the marriage from ending all those years ago. Until Davies intervened, we spared our little girl the pain, the humiliation from our unique circumstances.

"You might ask, why cheat on your wife with an identical woman? The answer is simpler than you imagine. Her sister was present. She was present when my wife — who was sexless — was preoccupied with other things. I was pitiful from the lack of sex. Hell, I only knew my junk still worked in the shower. I found myself alone one evening with her bodacious twin. A pleasant rye had loosened our nerves. We began whispering salacious things to each other. We were on each other like animals, Reg. I became addicted to the scintillating conversations, punctuated with lust. We were filthy.

"But I had to end the romance. We couldn't go on like that. It became too much as our families gathered for holidays and birthday parties. The twin looked over at me with flirtatious intentions from across the dining table. Just filthy. But I gave up the affair. I ended the romance with a carefully worded letter. I let her down easily. She didn't take it so well. She threatened vengeance. I thought she was bluffing, so I called her on it. She wasn't bluffing. She forwarded the letter to my wife. It all blew up in my face. I had no defense. Caught red-handed. So, I waited for my wife to tire of her rage. Little by little I began repairing the pieces of our tattered relationship. I can't say it has returned to the way it was before the affair, but the marriage survived. We saw our daughter off to college. Then I was elected mayor. I teased fate, grateful for my fortunes. And all at once, kismet returned with my public sentence. Now I shall return the favor to George Davies. There'll be no absolution for his sins. Come now, Reg, let us share a drink. A toast to sweet revenge."

After drinks, Reg set the plan in motion. He knew

people laundering money with George Davies. Reg was confident they'd kill Davies after learning he was stealing millions from them. Davies used Murphy's — the chain of fake Irish pubs — for cleaning money. Reg would pay an associate to make it appear cash had gone missing. They would tie this to George Davies. Some of it would be hidden in duffle bags at one of his properties. They'd use a place he rarely visited so he'd suspect nothing. The stolen money would be shown to the crooks through an anonymous lead. Like a pack of hounds, the angry beasts would be led to a trail that ended with Davies. They'd make him pay for the theft, sending a message to anyone else with double-crossing thoughts.

Reg knew no one would go to the feds. The scam built by Cheney and Davies was now running on autopilot. People were getting rich. Reg and Binks were making money from these schemes, and they weren't going to close the spigot. With Davies out of the way, not only would they have revenge, but they'd assume control of the entire enterprise. Charlie Cheney was dead. Davies would follow. Good fortune would return.

Binks followed the scheme's progress. On a few occasions, he'd suggest tweaking the plans. But he trusted Reg knew what he was doing. He wasn't sure how Reg became so competent in planning murders. He thought better of inquiring. The less information the mayor knew, the better. If this whole thing blew up, his ignorance could be the one thing to save his hide. The city was now engaged in the upcoming election. The disgraced mayor became yesterday's news which allowed him the space work outside of prying eyes. The journalists had moved on. His affair was a juicy story, but that story was old news. He was free to carry out his plan. Binks had Davies in his sights, aiming to cut him down.

15

Cremation and a Scheme at the Bank

L iam was alone in the apartment. The street below was busy and wet. Church Street was bustling with young professionals and tourists. One group with hurried impatience; the other lazy like frogs, hopping and scattering in search of the museum, shop, or place to eat. Rain was heavy, which cleared the way for cars pulling up, dropping off passengers who tried to avoid getting soaked. Liam sat near the kitchen staring at the ring box on the table. It felt untouchable. A reality he wanted but couldn't picture living.

He stressed over proposing to Maggie. This ring wasn't passed down from another generation. The singular history would begin here. With Maggie. A grandmother's ring would show some age. The wear and tear of life. Liam was staring at a blank canvas. A blank canvas has no direction. What if his first line is a mistake? He wanted a road map. Liam didn't want his parents' path. But it did show him what to avoid.

Liam now made his living as a writer. He played God with the characters he made—giving them life, siblings, death. Their lives hinged on his keystrokes. In the world outside of fiction, Liam couldn't control everything. He was nervous. Sure, she'd say yes. Sure?

His mind traveled to the dark possibility of rejection. What then? Sell the ring? Carry on as roommates? The cascading bad outcomes piled up inside his imagination. He thought about drinking, but it was too early for that. He set the box on the table, paced, stopping to look through the window over the wet street below. High up, everything looked small and massive at the same time. He shook the possibility of rejection from his head, picked up the box, placed it deep in a desk drawer.

Liam felt good now that he'd fleshed out the panic. He decided against writing a prepared speech. Instead, he'd improvise the proposal, riding the wave of the moment. Picturing it in his mind, he imagined Maggie smiling, blushing, crying all at the same time. He could hear her saying Yes. Repeating *Yes*. Then he heard the door open. Maggie entered.

"Liam?" She was soaked from the rain.

"In here," he said. Liam hid his anxiety with awkward movements. He kept a habit of rolling a pen around his fingers.

"Hey. I'm running errands for Gadly. Working from home the rest of the day. Caitlin is planning Charlie's cremation, so she asked me to deliver some work documents to her. At her house."

"What are your thoughts on cremation?" he asked.

"I'm not sure. I haven't thought about it."

"I think I want to be cremated when my time comes. The thought of being buried makes me feel claustrophobic."

"You'd be dead. You wouldn't notice a thing."

"What if I woke up? What if I'd fallen into a state unknown to the doctors? I looked dead for a moment, only to wake up after being buried. I'd scream without a chance of anyone hearing me. The lid of the coffin hovering above my face. I'd die from madness."

"At least you'd already be in a coffin," she said.

"How could you?"

"I'm helping you off the ledge. Save your outrageous scenarios for your books. Now I need to get out of these wet clothes." She left the room to change.

Liam turned back toward the kitchen. He thought more about Charlie's cremation. Maybe he should prepare a will. He'd never thought of it, but Charlie's death had been sudden. Less than a week ago, Liam was in London while Charlie was murdered in his own home. One never knows when the bill of death comes due. Liam was young but being young doesn't make you invincible. He began thinking about mortality after his father died, at times to an unhealthy degree. Now he worried about the suddenness with which death can arrive. At least with his father's experience, there was a diagnosis, then months to prepare. With Charlie, death came upon him in a surprise attack. His time stopped. No chance to dodge the permanent sleep or prepare the sheets.

Maggie called from the other room, asking Liam to come in. He found her naked. They smiled at each other as Liam removed his clothes. He kissed her and pressed her back against the wall. Maggie's hand moved below his stomach which made him skip a breath. They spent the afternoon in bed. Maggie forgot about the errands. Liam was no longer thinking about cremation.

The bank closed in fifteen minutes. Dan was stuck in traffic, unsure if he'd make it in time. He phoned Davies to tell him he was on the way, arriving soon. Dan's Uber pulled to the curb, nearly sending a cyclist to his death. He hopped out, fumbled with his phone, raced inside while his driver absorbed the abuse from the injured cyclist with a bent wheel. Dan was a disheveled wet mess when he met Davies inside the lobby.

"Benchman, you look like hell," Davies said. "No matter, let's get down to business." He led Dan to the office of Gus Tower, one of his associates. They shook hands. The meeting began.

"What can I help you with today, Georgie?" Gus asked.

"Dan Benchman here has an interest in joining the game. He's willing to invest a modest sum in our little business. Hell of a ballplayer in his youth. He was on his way to the big time until he smashed his shoulder. He never got his pitch back. Anyway, I've introduced Danny to a new game. A game for big boys. He'll be discreet. Let's get him on the register, Gussie."

Dan signed papers he didn't understand, depositing seventy-five thousand dollars into a new account. Gus said the funds would be invested in parking garages. Easy money. They used phrases like *passive income*. An introductory payment. It was Dan's path to building wealth. Real wealth. Gus spoke as though he wasn't a banker but a stakeholder in the business. It was confusing, by design. Dan didn't ask too many questions. Davies sat back in his chair, smiled, repeating things like, "Atta boy, Danny."

A young woman poked her head into the office. She was stylish and slim. Her hair was dark brown, short, and pomaded. Cat-eyeglasses on her nose, above sharp cheeks. Her beauty intimidated the three men in the room. She spoke with an accent. Might be German. Dan wasn't sure.

"Yes." Gus looked up.

"Done?" she asked.

"Getting close."

"I missed you the other night."

"I'm sure you did. I made other plans."

"Plans without me?"

"I'm sorry, but yes."

"Something occurred to me."

"Oh?"

"I think you owe me a favor. For the thing."

"What thing?"

"You know, the thing."

"Ah, yes. Forgive me."

"Shall I expect it... by the end of the week?"

"I suppose I can make that happen. This will help," replied Gus, pointing to Dan's paperwork.

"Sorry for the intrusion, gentlemen. Dan, it was good to make your acquaintance." The young woman left before Dan could answer. He didn't know how she knew his name. It was all so confusing but exciting at the same time. Dan thought, you only get ahead in life if you're willing to take chances. He and Michael pooled their money for this investment. Michael had received an inheritance from a distant relative he had never met. Dan also has access to his father's money. There was plenty to add to this initial payment. The proximity to wealth and power impressed Dan, desperate to join the club. It looked like Davies was going to win the election in a landslide. Dan wasn't about to spend the rest of his career in the minor leagues. With Davies, he felt like he was in the middle of an old-time mob movie. Dan started to behave with swagger. He was enjoying the Candidate's company. He couldn't bring himself to dine across the table from the grotesque figure, but in his company, he was beginning to feel his fortunes change. They had even discussed a plan to remove Gadly, leaving Davies in charge. Charlie had the misfortune of being poisoned to death. The Candidate needed an apprentice. Davies could use Dan. Dan had many talents. He was young and didn't come across like the lousy swindler most folks took Davies to be. Above all, Dan presented zero threat to Davies now with his money tied up in the game. If the boy becomes weak-kneed, Davies could threaten him with a lengthy jail sentence. Dan is no longer clean, and the only way for him to make real money from here out is to play dirty.

16

Confession and a Plan

Sunlight oozed along the outer edges of the curtains in Gadly's bedroom. Struggling to open his eyes, Gadly was especially tired this morning. The smell of fresh coffee pulled him out of bed quicker than he wanted. He put on his robe and found Caitlin in the kitchen. She was wearing only his dress shirt which fit her with chic looseness. They kissed good morning. She poured his coffee. He added milk, no sugar. They walked a few paces to a floral bench, seated by the window overlooking tall trees.

Caitlin said, "My guilt is killing me. Why don't I feel sadness over Charlie? Why *can't* I feel sad about him? Here I am, with you. Shouldn't I feel something? I feel like he never existed."

"You can't force emotions."

"I understand, but it can't be normal to feel nothing for your dead husband. And the way he went. So tragic. So violent. And yet, I don't have any remorse for Charlie. Dare I say, I'm happy he's gone. My marriage was an awful, awful prison."

Gadly paused. He wanted to be careful here. He

cleared his throat like a man seeking penance.

"It's selfish to say, but I'm happy you are here with me. Charlie was a dear friend, but I prefer our life now that he's gone. I don't mean to be callous."

Gadly stopped for a breath. Caitlin stared at his face. Charlie's death seemed tied to their affair, but she wasn't sure how.

Caitlin confessed, "I never loved him, you know. We rushed into the marriage because I was pregnant. We were so young. His parents wouldn't tolerate their first grandchild that way. I resented them for pressuring me into a marriage with a man I never loved. I resented myself for giving in to that pressure."

Her eyes looked down; her heart sank with them. "What is a life that longs for something you can't define? I wanted something else, but what, I didn't know. At least that's what I told myself. But I *did* know. I wanted to leave Charlie. I wanted out. I wanted him gone. But I was too scared to admit it because I knew I didn't have the courage to act."

Gadly spoke up. "Maybe what you've longed for is here. Am I mad for finding pleasure in this? What I mean to say is this: I am comforted in your arms. I am comforted in where we are now. What we have wouldn't be possible if Charlie was still alive."

Caitlin stared back at Gadly. Her face held two expressions, blurred. *Melpomene and Thalia.*

He continued. "Suppose I carry on with a guilty conscience. My wife was a good woman, but the truth is I didn't feel this way about her. Our marriage was fine. Nothing more. But with you, it's different. She was a kind woman, but I had grown tired of her. How can I speak this way of a dead woman? My wife.

"I hate to discard her as if she meant nothing to me. But it wasn't enough. After Marie died, Charlie helped me find happiness. He taught me to dream big. Then he ruined his marriage with you. That was his gift to me. That gift is you." Gadly wanted to take Caitlin's hand but didn't. "So, I loved you and made you laugh. You loved me back. I feel young again. My chest races in anticipation of touching you. I miss you when you aren't around.

"My marriage was a dull utility. I wasn't in love with Marie. If I'm being honest, I've always loved you. I imagined, the many times we dined at each other's home, what it would be like if the two of us could be together. When I kissed my wife, I wished it were you instead. Over the years, I dreamt of how your lips might taste. Here we are, on a clear path of freedom. A life together — me, free from banality — and you, free to laugh. Free to love. Just free."

Caitlin smiled. She looked at Gadly's face.

She said, "I thought of you often. But Marie was a friend. I hate to mention her name for the fear that guilt will keep me from loving you. But we moved on. We cannot look back. Those were the lives lived by the people we used to be. Let's leave those lives and those people behind. They are ghosts now."

Gadly put down his cup. He walked to the room. The drink was getting cold, untouched. The coffee and milk mixture hardened into a ridge near the lip of the mug. The mug was a gift from Marie. *Richard* was painted on the side in calligraphy. The dot was missing from the 'i', as if written in one stroke. A solitary name. A hermit hiding inside a marriage.

A pale white crossed his face. He was a man with a heavy heart.

"I… I must confess something more." He started slowly, then gained pace. "I killed a man. I murdered Charlie. I poisoned my friend," he said. His face was as white as chalk. "I killed him with savage bitterness in my heart. I took advantage of knowing my way around the house. I have been there a hundred times. I'm not a butcher, I made it clean. I made my way into the house, your house. I laid the trap. He died without sound. His final, fatal taste was his favorite Scotch. The glass was filled with ice, as he preferred. Relaxed, Charlie drifted into an eternal sleep. Two old friends—Brutus and Caesar. Like Caesar, Charlie was prone to tyranny. He raged on God while acting like a god. His tyranny spread to you. Oh, how I wanted him dead for that. No good for this world, removal was the only remedy.

"I could not live with the fear he might intervene in our affairs. I couldn't risk the possibility that someday you might have a change of heart and turn to him. That I could not allow. I could not bear it. I acted in self-defense. I mitigated the threat.

"You may hate me now. But do you see how free you are? The laughter you were deprived of was like keeping oxygen from your lungs. He cut off your oxygen, so I had to terminate his air so you could have yours. Wait. I can predict your questions. I can see it on your face. Where to from here? The answer is anywhere. Anywhere and everywhere. I murdered Charlie Cheney. Let God deal with his soul now."

Caitlin wasn't altogether surprised. She suspected Gadly but the confirmation brought her to a zenith of unpredictable panic. How was she to take this? Her husband's killer stands, confessed, a few feet away. Charlie's killer is also her liberator. She is free now that Charlie is dead. That much is true. What is also true is she shares her bed with a murderer.

In an instant, her mind takes a train far from this room. Her body is facing Gadly, but her thoughts are in a long, dark tunnel. Caitlin is now alone in the cabin, standing next to a tea cart. The cups are empty, but the pot is too hot to touch. The window is cracked open, the air outside cold. The blood running through her veins is freezing. Caitlin feels her face rushing in crimson as she struggles to breathe. She has left her body, now hovering above the train. The roof is covered with snow. She's traveling at such speed the icy wind cuts at her existence. She can't feel her hands or her feet. Gadly's white dress shirt is now a white dressing gown. It's torn and thin, nowhere near enough to keep her warm. Her flesh is exposed to the harsh conditions. How can she find warmth? She feels her soul harden like concrete drying in her limbs. Trying to bend her knees, she notices they are covered in blood. She wants to scream but knows it's futile. Caitlin sees a vision of an older man holding a baby. It's a baby girl. It's Rebecca. Charlie swaddles her. He kisses her head as she looks into his eyes. They cannot see Caitlin. The closer she gets to her family, the farther they move away. It's a winless game. Caitlin thrusts her arms as if to swim through the cold, thick air to her family. She wants to hold her daughter. She wants to see Rebecca alive. She cannot. Caitlin closes her swollen eyes. She blubbers but makes no sound. The more she cries, the harder it becomes to catch her breath. She's now reaching for air. The train increases speed, and so does she. It feels out of control. Everything, out of control. Ahead is a tunnel; it's approaching with even more speed. Caitlin cannot move. She cannot avoid the hard stone of reality and must face it head-on. In this part of the play, she can only watch as an audience member fixed on the plot's next move. The tunnel is on her now as her eyes close. She braces for impact. A sharp pain races to the back of her head. It brings her to. She's dizzy. Her vision is blurred. Caitlin sees a shadow standing over her. He's screaming her name, but there's no clarity in the voice. Her eyes roll back into her head; darkness arrives.

Hours pass before she wakes. When Caitlin opens her eyes, she doesn't recognize the room. She attempts to focus her eyes on the sunlight peeking by the curtains.

Caitlin is still silent as someone enters the room. It's Gadly. A doctor is with him. The doctor checks her vital signs, she submits. Too weak to ask questions. The doctor speaks to Gadly, but she can't make out the conversation. Her ears are ringing. The sound drives a sharp pain straight onto the top of her head. The crushing headache is relentless. The doctor leaves. Caitlin reaches for her head, feeling a bandage. Gadly sits down in front of her.

"Caitlin, can you hear me?"

She nods but she's weak. He brings a cup of cold water to her lips. She drinks what she can. Gadly wipes the excess from her chin. He rubs her arm.

"You passed out yesterday morning. We were drinking coffee and talking. Your legs buckled and your head smashed against the table on the way to the floor. You were unresponsive, so I called 911. You have a concussion and need to rest. You gave me a good scare."

"We were talking about..." She struggled to collect her thoughts.

"It's not important right now. Please rest."

"Wait."

"Yes, dear."

"What did you say to me? What made me fall?"

"Not now. The doctor says you need to rest. Here, take these. They will help you sleep."

He placed two pills in her hand. She washed them down with water. In a short while, she fell asleep—a peaceful sleep. Gadly left the room. The headache was gone.

17

How the Game is Played

The bedroom was dark, a little past three in the morning when Liam's phone rang, smashing through his sleep: Jack was calling from London.

"Hello," he croaked.

"You awake?"

Maggie rolled over, closer to Liam, her head against his neck. She could hear Jack's voice shouting through the phone.

"I married Abam."

"What? Really?"

"Yes, last night in London. No fuss."

Liam was now awake.

"Um, wow. Congratulations. To you both. We love Abam."

"I feel like I'm walking on air." Jack said. He started talking about love like it was a thing few people knew about. Something he found in shale rock, dug up with a flat chisel. True love from a fling. Fossil from rock. Abam made him a better man, he said.

"There was much to improve on."

"I'm serious."

"So am I."

"It's your turn now. Have you asked Mag—"

Liam cut him off, jumped out of bed, away from Maggie's ear. Whispering now from the other room, he pleaded, "Shh, she's lying next to me. She'll hear you."

"What are you waiting for?"

"I want it to be a surprise, but now isn't the best time. I told you Maggie's overwhelmed with work. And she's dealing with Davies. Soon."

"Abam and I signed a lease on a flat in Camden. I may list my house in LA. You and Maggie should buy it."

"We're not buying your house. We can't afford it. We're not moving to Los Angeles."

"LA is great."

"Then why sell the house?"

"The city's not what it used to be. Hollywood bullshit."

Liam laughed. He enjoyed Jack's bold lack of self-awareness.

"We can't wait to have you guys over to our new place. We'll order in. Do our best to move you here."

"So no more LA then?"

"Fuck LA."

"Ha, ha. Perfect."

"I met this guy with a vintage wine collection. Decent prices. Anyway, he gave us some nice bottles."

"You always have... *a guy*. But I need to sleep now."

"Listen, you gotta ask Maggie to marry you. Don't wait."

"So now you're doling out relationship advice?"

"I know a good woman when I see one. Maggie is a good woman."

"Thanks for the revelation."

"All right, Shake. Abam and I are heading out."

Abam's soft voice snuck in, "Hello," in a rare moment Jack wasn't speaking.

"Congratulations. We are so happy for you both."

"Thanks, dear. While I have you, the show is progressing, and the studio is pleased. The early footage is exquisite."

"A relief to hear. Thank you so much. I can't imagine this project without you."

"It's a powerful story. Now go to sleep. We are off."

"Good night."

"Night."

Liam returned to bed to find Maggie awake. He told her about Jack and Abam's quick marriage. She was happy for them, excited to celebrate in person. They spent the early morning talking about their own wedding day. Debated having something big and traditional, or going off somewhere unannounced, like Jack and Abam. No family. No pressure. She nudged him, joking that she'd have to be the one to propose. He jabbed back that she'd have to divorce Gadly first.

Then Maggie changed the subject.

"I need to tell you something."

"Okay." Liam wasn't sure where this was going.

"I'm having issues with Davies. At the office."

"You said he's a creep. And corrupt."

"It's not that. I mean, yes, he's corrupted. He's probably a criminal. But that's not what I'm talking about."

"What is it?"

"I don't know where to start." Maggie sat up, covering herself with a sheet. Her eyes looked ill.

"It began with small comments. Kind of creepy but not a big deal. Like how he likes the way I dress. He likes my shoes."

"Yeah…"

"Then he started hanging out in my office. Hanging around my desk longer than he needed to. The usual chats turned from sharing recipes to what I'm wearing or something about my body. He'll do it right in front of Dan. And Gadly. They don't say anything."

"They don't say anything because Davies is too important."

"Exactly. But it doesn't end there. Davies makes demands of me. He orders me to fetch him lunch or to run errands for him. I'm not his assistant. He wants to humiliate me. But now he's crossed a line I cannot ignore."

"What did he do?"

"He touched me." Maggie stopped. Liam gave her space to collect her thoughts. "We were in the kitchen.

He moved past me, sliding his hand up my leg and over my ass. He left his hand there. It seemed like forever. Maybe a few seconds. What I do know is it wasn't an accident. Like I was just standing there waiting for him."

Liam couldn't speak.

"It's gross. I'm made to feel like meat. I can see it in the way he looks at me. Gadly and Dan must see it too, but they don't say anything because they need Davies. They need him more than they need me. I'm expendable. I know it. I have no power, no agency. I cannot even go to work without being reminded I'm worthless." She started to cry. Crying made Maggie hate the situation even more.

Liam put his arms around her. He didn't know what to say and chose to say nothing. Maggie pressed her hands against his back, pulling Liam in tighter. Warmth ran through the sheet that covered her body. She felt the strength of his back, it made her feel safe. But this was short-lived as she turned her mind back to George Davies.

Maggie wiped her face and continued. "There are things I deal with at work that you will never understand. You can't understand." Maggie got up from bed. She picked up a T-shirt from the floor and put it on. Looking outside, she became lost in two squirrels chasing each other up a tree. Flirting and fighting. She couldn't distinguish whether they were both enjoying the game or was one or the other running for their life.

Then she turned back to face Liam.

"I have three choices here: I can keep quiet, or I can speak up and they'll replace me with someone less noisy; or I quit my job.

Sorry, I do have a fourth option: I say something and be made to feel like I'm hysterical. Like I must have misinterpreted the situation: 'Maggie, don't flatter yourself. I don't want to flirt *with you*. Darling, you can't assume everyone wants you. Don't be so enamored with yourself.'

"Should I choose Door Three, I'd have to leave and look for another job. And Davies will carry on with the same depraved behavior. I don't want to be a victim.

"The new 'Maggie' will have to accept it. All of it. She'll bear the dehumanizing behavior. The comments. She'll be stuck with the same options. Which is to say, she'll have no options. Zero options to match zero consequences for George Davies."

Liam, a man of words, didn't have words for this situation. He felt angry, helpless. He was ashamed for being aloof to what Maggie had been going through at her job. The TV show consumed him. He didn't protect her. He wanted to strike Davies like an animal. He imagined himself choking the life from the pig.

"You have to say something."

"Fuck, Liam. You're not listening to me. I feel like no one is listening to me. It's like I'm the only one who can see what's going on around here. With everything. All the chaos. The corruption. I keep saying something, but nothing changes. But this, I can't say anything."

"He can't get away with this."

"He gets away with it because the world broke long ago, and in this office, I don't have the power to fix it. I don't have power here. Gadly made it really clear to me with his silence. These things happen Right. In. Front of him. Right there. Dan too. They say nothing. Nothing." She was fuming. "I was afraid to bring this up because I don't want to mess things up for you. I already feel like shit. What if something I say ruins your project? I have no choice but to absorb it. I will take it for you."

"I can't let you do that. I don't care about the show. There'll be others."

"You don't know that. A break like this won't happen with everything you write. What about Jack and Abam? How would a failed project affect them?"

"We'll get funding from somebody else."

"Where? Who? It doesn't work that way, and you know it."

Liam had no solutions. He was paralyzed by his inability to fix the situation.

"We'll get through this. I can handle Davies. I had to get this out. It was killing me inside."

"How can I carry on with the show knowing what you're dealing with? This is impossible."

"I'll work to keep Davies off me. As the election gets close, his schedule will be overwhelmed with appearances. I'm responsible for managing those appearances, so I'll keep him busy. Finish the show.

Let's make it a success. Then leave this place."

"We can go to New York. Or London."

"Anywhere but here."

Liam paused. "Are you sure this is what you want to do?"

"I'm sure. But I need you to be strong. It's the only way this will work."

"I hope you're right."

"I'm so proud of you. I want this for you. I believe in you. I need you to do the same for me. Do you believe in me? Do you believe I can handle this?"

"I do believe in you. I always have."

"It's for us. I'll be fine. I love you."

"I love you, but I hate this."

"Focus on what we need right now."

Maggie returned to bed. The sun was up. They lay in silence as the room lit up with the new day. Deep in thought, they wondered separately what the future held. Maggie was gaining strength after letting out what she had bottled inside for so long. Liam was anxious. He was vacillating between feeling upset for Maggie and his contempt for George Davies.

18

Candidate Trapped

The plan was set in motion, approved by Mayor Binks. Reg was aware of two men Davies used to smuggle money. With a threat to their lives, he'd convince them to hand the money over to his henchmen. Reg's men would beat the smugglers, leaving enough of a mark to guarantee their understanding of the situation. As Reg called them, The Men would use their contact, Gus Tower, who had a controlling interest in an offshore bank, to feed the money into several accounts traced back to George Davies. Another stash would be hiding on a property he rarely visited. They'd leave a trail to trace the stolen cash straight to Davies. The trail would be made discoverable to stakeholders in the shell companies. He'd have nowhere to run.

Gus had an associate, a young woman named Anna, who would bring the damning information to the stakeholders. She is who met Dan that day in Gus's office, the day Dan's account was set up with Davies.

Anna, a smart woman with a dizzying collection of passports, spoke many languages. Like a character out of a spy novel, she could disappear once inside a border. She traveled the world cloaked in invisibility, protected by influential people. Anna was famous for double-crossing the double-crossers. Uncatchable because she was untraceable. Gus Tower wasn't sure Anna was even her real name. Gus became romantically involved with her last year. Out of fear of the romance ending, he chose not to ask questions. When they made love, she was always on top. He thought there was something to that. Anna's tactics were no business of his, he said.

The first transfer Gus went after was the money coming from Dan Benchman's investment. Dan was harmless. The original intent of his money was to be used to invest in downtown parking garages and lots. This scheme created a legitimate account which Davies planned to use as a haven for dirty money. The Men would take the profits from Dan's investment, then Gus would put that money in an offshore account belonging to George Davies. Anna delivered the paper trail. Because Gus also worked with Davies, the Candidate wouldn't suspect why a batch of new funds showed up in his bank account. Reg relished the simplicity of the scheme. A straight line is easy to follow. Moving money from right under the Candidate's nose was the play because his avarice would betray his senses. Both Reg and Mayor Binks blissed in the poetic justice of cutting Davies down by using his own schemes against him. Gus brought with him trust from both sides of the game. Like a skilled magician, Anna could show the hand, then take it away while the eye was distracted. Before you could ask the magician to reveal her trick, she'd disappear, unreachable across a new border.

Gus kept Dan Benchman satisfied by dumping parking garage profits into his account. Blinded by fast, easy money. The primary goal here for Gus was to use Dan as a cash canal. He then convinced Dan to open a line of credit to carry on with the extensive remodel of his house. The debt was created, which further entrenched Dan into the game. Now he couldn't leave. Gus provided him with easy money from the parking garages and a line of credit to live above his means. In return, Dan ended up owing the bank a sum of money worth more than his mortgage. Gus had woven a silky web for the former pitcher. Dan was stuck. It was bases loaded in a tie ballgame, and Dan couldn't throw a strike if his life depended on it. But in this game, his life, indeed, depended on it.

Davies employed men to transport the funds, hidden in the back of an air conditioner repair truck. The pair of goons driving the truck were high on fast food, with the reassuring feeling of being, if not above the law, well outside it. Reg's men had set up roadworks thirty miles before the state line, between Kentucky and Tennessee. The air conditioner repair truck would be allowed through the barricade and the traffic behind them would be stopped. The stoppage created an empty stretch of highway for Reg's men to do their job. The goons enjoyed a touch of schadenfreude at the poor saps stuck behind them in traffic purgatory. The trap was set.

Reg's men, driving a bogus state trooper's car, diverted the repair truck off the road, miles away from even a gas station. No witnesses, nowhere to hide. They hijacked the air conditioner repair truck and beat the goons to within an inch of their lives. After the beating, one 'trooper' drove away in the repair truck and the other fled the scene in the fake police car. Reg's men were now in possession of the assets. Because he was a man of symmetry, Gus had arranged for them to make the drop at the same garage where Dan Benchman parked his investment. Anna took care of the surveillance cameras inside the garage. She then took possession of the funds and drove to the airport to leave the country. Reg's men retired the stolen repair truck to a junkyard outside of town. As it happens, a junkyard run by a used car dealer whose dealership is another place Davies managed to wash money. As if to twist the knife in the Candidate's back, Mayor Binks intended to use the complex system Davies created to enrich himself to bite the hand that fed him.

Anna made her way to Seychelles. Gus arranged a meeting with the bank officer who would deposit the intercepted cash, signed by George Davies. Anna was a master at forgery. Davies signed his name like a child in an earthquake. It was easy to copy.

The total sum of money was four million dollars. The deposits would occur incrementally, to elude suspicion. The initial phase of the plan was now complete. The next stage would be to alert the stakeholders to the missing funds. This phase was tricky. Gus knew he needed to proceed with caution. He would start by leading them to the cash hidden at an address belonging to Davies. Gus Tower is a cunning fellow, but even a shrewd virtuoso, one trained in the dark arts of money laundering and self-dealing, must remain vigilant. One wrong move, one single lapse of judgment would mean a direct death sentence of his effecting. Any death sentence is an unfortunate circumstance. The death sentences in this world hold a particular kind of cruelty. They include a dose of torture before the execution. Or, if the executioner likes, it may consist of torture within the act itself. For example, Gus could find himself thrown from the top of a tall building with plenty of time to terrify his mind before his life is cut short upon impact. It's not enough to deal with a problem. An exclamation point must accompany the removal. A deterrent.

Days later, Gus sat in his office, drinking whiskey, and working. As the drink warmed his throat and chest, he became pleased with his recent accomplishments. The first half of the scheme was hitchless.

The phone rang. It was Anna who was now in Berlin. She was seated at the end of the bar, in the lobby of the Michelberger Hotel. She confirmed to Gus that the job was done without interruption.

"The officer in Seychelles is discreet?" she asked.

"Yes. He is a reliable partner."

"Is there anyone on the team you think capable of betrayal?"

"It's always possible in this business. But I've chosen each player carefully."

"How about Reg's men? Can they be trusted? I imagine they could be paid off. I like to think of them as partners with wandering eyes. Always on the hunt for something more attractive."

"Sure, the right sum of money can awaken their vapid minds. Should they be tempted to cross us, we'll put our foot down on them as well. If necessary."

He poured another glass. The whiskey made him loose, which, at the same time, lowered his reliable defenses. He began speaking in flirtatious tones.

"When are you coming back to America, sweetie? I miss you already."

"Soon. I return soon."

"Have you thought of leaving this life? We can start over on the other side of the world. We can go anywhere. I'll meet you in Switzerland. Settle in the Alps. A simple life, but one filled with the finest luxuries. I will spoil you."

"You do spoil me. You have given me more than you know."

"That is kind of you to recognize."

"Even you are not aware of how much you've given me."

"How so?"

"I have secured everything you've accumulated

through your endeavors. There is one more thing I need from you."

"You've secured everything?" He was confused and drunk. "What are you talking about? What final thing?"

"Your life."

The door to his office opened with a thud. Reg's men came rushing into the room. Gus tried to stand but was forced back down onto his leather chair. Anna remained on the line.

"I need you to write the following note…"

With a handgun pressed against his temple, Gus, trembling, wrote:

I schemed to embezzle millions of dollars from my clients. George Davies, my trusted partner, and I have become rich through these schemes. I have spent most of my life defrauding people who put their financial trust in me. I robbed them of their life savings. I have stolen from their investments. I used stolen earnings to create profits for myself outside the boundaries of acceptable fiduciary duties. A disgrace, I cannot live with myself any longer. My depravity has consumed my will to live. It is with a heavy conscience that I choose to end my life. May God have mercy on me.

Regretfully,
Gus Tower

Gus Tower hung from his office door with his tie. His shoes had been removed. Anna scrapped the burner phone; Reg's men exited the building without notice. Word made its way back to Reg that Gus Tower was dead. Reg explained to Mayor Binks that this was a necessary part of the plan. He couldn't risk Gus, in a drunken stupor, divulging secret information. Gus was famous for talking too much. There was a recent episode when he confided with Reg about wanting out of the game. He talked about going away with Anna, to live a happy life free from the chaos of crime. Reg tried to reason with him. Gus didn't even know this woman's real name. Did he not stop imagining her cunning ways being used against him? His passion for Anna blinded him to the most obvious possibility. Gus was broken inside. Only broken men pursue a life of crime. Only a fractured man can steal with a smile on his face. Gus couldn't take it *as it was*. He thought he could fix it himself. The fix would include a quiet life, outside the fray, with Anna. His weeping heart, from years of thieving, was desperate for a reprieve. Gus convinced himself he could wash away his sins by refraining from future crimes. The warmth he felt from Anna's pretended affections, in his corrupted mind, would cancel his evil deeds. Instead, he faced a violent ending, hung by a satin tie, betrayed by his associates in a scheme to betray his clients. The trust he abused came back like a karmic lash around his neck in the same office he came to work in each day, doing criminal business. Fate showed enough benevolence to allow time for one last taste of expensive whiskey. The relaxing drink did its job, preparing him for an exit from his crimes. Not the way he intended but so it was. Gus Tower was now a hung man.

19

Rebecca and the Pink Sky

Traced to Rivqah, a Hebrew name meaning to join or tie, Rebecca's existence was meant to bind. Caitlin's unexpected pregnancy in college forced a quick marriage with Charlie, forever linking the two otherwise opposite young students. Rebecca's death initiated another bond, keeping two grieving parents together, though they lived separate lives. Caitlin used to fantasize about what Rebecca's life would have been like had she survived birth. Caitlin spent time inventing scenes of mother and daughter marking important achievements in the child's life. She imagined the baptism. A lighted Christmas tree surrounded by gifts. Birthdays or school events. Anything to do with childhood. Caitlin didn't picture an adult Rebecca. She remained a child. The impossibility of Rebecca growing up was stubborn even in Caitlin's dreams.

The daydreams appeared in her night dreams. Like visions. So vivid were these visions that Caitlin would spend the following day heartbroken after waking up to find she was only dreaming. She longed for sleep where she could escape into Rebecca's world. An enchanted world. In it, Charlie appeared nowhere. His name never mentioned. In this fantasy world, Rebecca didn't long for her father. No sad faces here. Rebecca's heart was filled with her mother's love. In Caitlin's subconscious patchwork inventions, Rebecca was alive, wise, helpful. Rebecca brought calm to Caitlin's anxiety, by fixing the impossible.

A particular episode appeared in Caitlin's dreams. Myth theater with a familiar arc. In a magical world, Rebecca possessed the ability to cure sadness. The scene began in a small English village, with rolling green hills dotted by cottages and thatch roofing. A rainbow drew across the sky though it never rained in this version of England. The cloudless sky was an infinite source of light. Its shade of blue was a color Caitlin didn't recognize. The sky looked like a child's blanket, soft and secure: an air-puffed shell protecting the villagers below it, uncorrupted by harsh weather. The fields never fell into darkness after Rebecca was born. She was an angelic child.

Early on, the locals didn't detect her gift for reversing sadness. In the earliest examples, it was explained away, not as supernatural, but instead by her kind disposition. The people of the village talked of the joy Rebecca brought everyone. Caitlin did not appear in the dream, she was only an observer, but Rebecca did know her audience as she delivered messages of joy from a faraway world.

A young boy in the village became inconsolable

after his dog died. His dog had fallen ill, and the sickness passed quickly through its body. As the boy buried the dog in a field near the family home, Rebecca went out to meet him. She was fourteen at the time. He was found weeping, on his knees in a field of English daisies. Rebecca approached, knelt beside him, rested her soft hand on his shoulder without saying a word. The boy looked in the sun's direction, though not directly. He saw a vision in the bright sky. The sky turned from blue to pink. In the vision there was a montage of the child playing with his dog, running the fields, throwing sticks, rolling around while the pup licked his face. As Rebecca looked at her hand, she spotted a sparkling mist dancing around it, above the boy's shoulder. He stopped crying as he focused his mind on the cherished years playing with his dog. Instead of loss, he saw only a life lived. Rebecca couldn't bring back the dog, but she could make the boy see that though the body had gone, the experiences did not fade. Time waters age with wrinkles, decay. But the spirit lives on—beyond the reach of clocks. A loyal friend. Unconditional. The dog made him happy. The boy's happiness was still real. And so was his dog.

In another dream, a peasant of old age near the end of his life sat reflecting in his fields. He led a solitary existence surrounded by crops and work. Never married, without children, he was clogged in isolation. The old man spent hours in his fields thinking of the road not taken. In a parallel life, he was married with five children: two sons, three daughters. His children grew up to help toil in the fields, providing food and sustainability for the village. The additional hands produced more food for more families. He would pass his life's work onto his children. And on and on into future generations of peasants providing food for their villages and neighboring towns.

Rebecca found him showered in the sadness of being childless. Spouseless. The abruptness of death concentrated his mind. There was no one to carry on with his crops. They'd waste away from neglect, choked out by the weeds, ravaged by wild animals. As Rebecca came nearer to the peasant, she sang a sweet hymn in his ear:

Let the lower lights be burning!
Send a gleam across the wave!
Some poor fainting, struggling seaman
You may rescue, you may save.

Trim your feeble lamp, my brother;
Some poor sailor, tempest-tossed,
Trying now to make the harbor,
In the darkness may be lost.

She paused here. Watching as the peasant fell to his knees. Looking up toward the sky, now pink, he wailed, not in despair, instead lit with joy. She repeated the following refrain:

Let the lower lights be burning!
Send a gleam across the wave!
Some poor fainting, struggling seaman
You may rescue, you may save.

A vision appeared of families enjoying the harvest, feeding their children. He watched a loop of his work sustain perfect strangers. Those children may not have a blood relation to the peasant, but he saw a new type of offspring; one sprung forward with the crops he raised. Without his toil, the villagers could not eat. Couldn't live. Or bring up children so their stories and lives would go on. Rebecca lifted the veil of sadness to reveal how the peasant had touched so many lives. The dirt under his nails had a purpose. The worn soles of his boots carried a weight bigger than his body. The physical pain brought about by his labor removed the hunger pangs from the bellies of starving children. His work in the early morning hours provided a table of food for the villagers' evening meals.

Rebecca's gift allowed him to see this. He was content, proud. When it was time for him to die, he closed his eyes, knowing his work was finished, and he felt the weight of his body press into the ground. Conscious of his final breath, he let go.

The village held a ceremony for him. Rebecca was there. They wrapped his body in soft sheets and carried him to his burial site, at the edge of the land. Children sang songs thanking him for his work. They thanked him for providing food for their families. After the funeral, they divided responsibilities between them, continuing his work for generations.

Rebecca fell to tears and the little girl found herself confused. Was she crying because she was sad? How could she feel happy at the same time? Caitlin wanted to run to her but could not. Her mother was only allowed to watch because that's how dreams work. Caitlin wept as she was dismayed by impotence. The village emptied, and Rebecca was left alone in the field. The sky returned to a shade of blue. But no longer clear blue. The sky was now turning gray. The kind of dark gray that shows an incoming storm. The clouds swirled and moved in a chaotic waltz. Chaos replaced the calm. Pink-Blue-Gray. 1-2-3.

Rebecca continued to cry. Alone. She was now wounded by sadness. The dreamland prevented Caitlin from helping her daughter. Reaching, Caitlin grabbed only emptiness. She wanted to hold Rebecca. She prayed to reverse the sadness in her child's heart. She could not. The mother, paralyzed in a REM cycle, screamed without sound. Her legs wouldn't, couldn't move her. For the first time in this dream series, darkness draped the fields. Rebecca disappeared into the landscape. She was no more. Caitlin could not bear this as she felt her life shattering to pieces. The pain of loss shot straight to her heart. Then the other voices came as the room filled with doctors and nurses. She saw fluorescent lights overhead. The equipment was cold. The doctors moved with frantic attention. She heard Charlie's voice though she didn't see his face. There was a baby. Then there was silence.

Caitlin woke up, lying on a sofa in her home. Her cheeks were wet with tears. The room was mostly black except for a lamp in the far corner. She sat up, covered herself with a blanket but still felt frozen in her bones. Caitlin took a few moments to gather herself, then left the sofa like a skittish ghost and walked to Rebecca's bedroom. A night light projecting a pink moon on the ceiling lit the child's vacant bed. Wrapped in the blanket, Caitlin walked to the rocking chair. She picked up a teddy bear Odette had mailed from France. She sat, pressing the bear against her chest. She slept.

Caitlin never pictured herself growing old with Charlie, always divergent paths. When vacationing in another country, she'd explore the city alone. Charlie was either too tired or too distracted with work for tourism. Once, in Milan, she ordered a coffee and walked about the town on her own. She pretended she was walking alongside an attentive lover. Their conversations flowed seamlessly and easily. He lifted Caitlin's hair behind her ear, to see her face. Dote when she wasn't doing anything extraordinary. When they'd come across a street musician, he'd drop a few notes in the money jar — unembarrassed in the crowd — take her in his arms to dance beneath the light post. He'd talk about selling everything and buying a place on Lake Como for a quiet life together. The imaginary partner hung on to her words as she retold stories. In the middle of a story, he'd remember something she said last month because he always listened. To the strangers passing by on the avenue, she looked happy as she smiled and drank coffee. The locals were unaware she was playing make-believe, pretending to walk the streets of Italy with her neat, handsome lover.

Back at the hotel, she was shot back to reality at the sight of Charlie, in thin-rimmed glasses and ill-fitting clothing, shouting into a cell phone. The lights were off even though the sun was setting, adding to the scene's utter drabness. Cut off from the architecture, history, and radiant life outside, she sat on the bed waiting for him to finish work as she stared at his open suitcase and the clothes he'd strewn about the floor. Sometimes she'd give up, go downstairs to the bar where she'd order a glass of red wine — any red wine would do — and strike up a conversation with the bartender or an attractive couple nearby. The nights were lonely, building a solid case for leaving Charlie. She didn't know how or when she'd divorce him. But their separation was inevitable. She was eager for that time to arrive. Caitlin had already quit the marriage in her mind and in her heart. Her legs were finding the courage to remove her from this hell. What wasn't visible then was Charlie's impending death.

One day Caitlin decided to get rid of things in her house. She emptied the closets and the attic. Anything she hadn't seen or thought about in over a year had to go. She wasn't precious about it. She approached the effort without nostalgia. Cleaning out the surplus had an almost medicinal effect on her mind. She could feel her thoughts reaching clarity with each box hauled away. We can't reduce her efforts to only a spring-cleaning ritual, though that's not inaccurate. She was preparing for something bigger. She was preparing to leave her husband.

The recurring dreams of Rebecca were a lesson. Her daughter was showing her there was a way out. Tearing apart the marriage would be a necessary start to building a new life. Caitlin had to face this uncomfortable truth. She had to leave the house, everything it represented. She must leave Rebecca's room behind. Her daughter never occupied that space, but she does visit her mother in her dreams. She could take Rebecca with her anywhere. To another country. To the beach or the mountains. She'd accompany her mother for walks on a busy weekday in Milan. When Rebecca was old enough, Caitlin imagined buying her a coffee, renting a car, driving to the water to laugh at their reflections on the lake. They'd take pictures at sunset, stay up late drinking wine on the patio after dinner. Rebecca would try exotic foods. Some she'd like and some she wouldn't care for.

This combination of dream and make-believe may sound pathetic to some: the detached reality of a woman gone mad. Caitlin saw it as a temporary limbo. A period of transit, leaving the misery that is her life with Charlie for a chance at a new beginning. The unknown excited Caitlin. And Rebecca's spirit made her feel invincible.

20

An Unraveling

An emergency meeting was called. Dan and Maggie rushed to the conference room to join Gadly and Davies who were already waiting. Caitlin was in the office though she didn't join the others. Gus Tower's suicide was all over the news. Davies was troubled, but not because of compassion for his friend. Gus was an ally who assisted Davies with his schemes. Anna robbed both men.

Davies was now in need of four million dollars which belonged to the angry associates breathing down his neck, wanting their money. He didn't know that the disgraced mayor, Binks, was behind the scenes orchestrating the whole affair.

People were asking Davies about the four million in missing cash. His campaign's internal polling showed his numbers falling as the air of corruption followed his name. Donors pressured him to quit the race while they still had time to find a replacement. Davies was choking with anxiety with his chances of being elected nearing zero. The pressure on his life to find the missing money was unbearable. He sought guidance from Gadly but couldn't be truthful because that required him to admit to his crimes.

Gadly advised Davies to leave the race. An easy, though unfortunate, fix to one of his two major dilemmas. He needed to prioritize his troubles, and if he was elected these issues would handicap his administration. The high office would only shine a spotlight on his corruption charges. There was no other way forward.

Stubborn, Davies was conditioned to never admit defeat. He and Gadly spent the next hour arguing whether he'd remain in the race. When the conversation moved to the missing money, Davies changed the subject. He couldn't come clean with the truth, which meant there would be no chance of a resolution.

Maggie was relieved to know Davies would not be Nashville's next mayor. Whether he dropped out or not, Davies was finished. There would be no need for Gadly's services with him out of the race, which meant she could remove the stench of George Davies from her professional life. These events wouldn't affect Liam's show because Davies had already invested the money. Jack and Abam could deal with Davies should he get difficult. He was losing power. George Davies was trapped under the weight of his own corruption.

Gadly began a line of questioning.

"George, how long has Gus been embezzling money?"

"I don't know."

"The four million… where did it come from?"

"Investments. My investments."

"That's a lot of money."

"It has nothing to do with this race."

"The race is over, George. I think you know that."

"Fuck you, Gadly."

"I'm always straight with you. That's why you hired me."

"I hired you to get me elected. Now I need you to fix this."

Gadly paused for a breath. "I can't fix it. I have no idea what the hell is going on here. You're lying to us about this affair. We can't advise you in the dark."

"My investments have nothing to do with you."

"They do now because it's affecting the election. This whole thing is a mess. The FBI is moving on this. I need you to tell us what is going on here."

"Don't say anything to the cops." Davies was spitting.

"I can't say anything to them because I have no idea what you're up to."

"Gus and I were working with investors from overseas. They helped with my business. I do a lot of business. They helped get BioPharma Manufacturing off the ground—the company I created with Charlie. The company responsible for propping up *this* firm. Gus didn't take money from me; he stole it from the investors. Several duffle bags of cash were found on one of my properties. A place I rarely visit. It's a wonderful place though. I should see it more often. A lot of money was found in those bags but not enough. They're after me. Dirty little hounds. I don't have access to four million dollars, so I must find out what Gus did with it, or I'm a dead man."

Gadly stopped asking questions. He felt, for his protection, it was better if he didn't know the details.

"George, our work here is finished. I'm no longer advising you on any future matters."

"Who do you think you are?"

"I'm sorry. It must be this way."

Davies stood up. His reddish face became more bloated than usual. His skin looked like a spoiled onion.

"Cowards." He stormed out of the office. The room went silent.

Maggie felt ill; she was in the middle of something sick. Dan excused himself and ran after Davies. He had opened an account with Gus Tower and was concerned his money might be missing too. Gadly needed to speak with Caitlin. He went upstairs to her office and closed the door behind him. Maggie was left alone in the conference room. She wondered how much Gadly knew or how much he was pretending not to know. Charlie Cheney was his closest friend. Did he know Charlie created illegal schemes with Davies? What about Charlie's murder? What does Caitlin know? Maggie felt claustrophobic as she became surrounded by crooks and murderers. She sat unmoved, trying to breathe. Panic would do her no good in this situation. She climbed the stairs to retrieve her purse, shut down her computer, and left without turning off the lights. She overheard Gadly and Caitlin having a conversation but didn't stop to listen. As she made her way down the stairs, the front door opened. Dan returned.

"Are you heading out?" he asked. He looked panicked.

"Yes. I need to leave for the day. I'm not sure what's just happened here, but I know I need to leave."

"Where's Gadly?"

"Upstairs, with Caitlin."

"I'll let you know what I find out."

Maggie left without saying goodbye. She crossed the street without looking. Her head was spinning. She raced home.

Inside Caitlin's office, the discussion was intense.

"What do you propose?" Caitlin said.

"Davies has to go."

"Didn't you fire him already?"

"Yes."

"Did he agree to leave the race?"

"Not so much. But that part doesn't matter. He has no chance at winning now."

"Then what's the problem?"

"The FBI will be asking questions. Charlie and George were laundering money and I'm worried more questions will be asked regarding Charlie's death."

"That case is closed."

"It could be re-opened. How much do you know

about Charlie's business?"

"Not much. Swampy, but not criminal."

"Well, it *was* criminal."

"I had no idea, did you?"

"Not right away. But I learned as much when Davies came around. I thought I could get away with poisoning Charlie because, at some point, his crimes would come to light. Once the cops realized he was laundering money, it would be anyone's guess who might have done it."

"Why are you worried now?"

"Because his crimes are now bearing down on me. On us. We don't need the cops sniffing around for clues to an unsolved murder case."

"What's to be done?"

"Davies must be handled. I gotta kill him."

"No. No more killing."

"It's the only way, Caitlin."

She was panicking. "The killing must stop. This is out of control. I can't bear it."

"I will handle this. I'll keep you in the dark for your protection."

He held her. Caitlin's body was rigid.

Dan left the office and was on his way to the bank. He needed to know his money was safe. When he arrived, he was surprised to see George Davies in the lobby.

"Benchman. I'm glad to see you."

"Oh, I didn't expect you here."

"You know the account Gus Tower created for you, the investment into our little parking business?"

"Yes. That's why I'm here."

"I anticipated you might be worried. Your money is safe. Gus made you rich."

Dan was relieved, either too stupid or too smart to ask questions.

"Danny, I need you to do me a favor here."

"How can I help?"

"I promised I'd make you a rich man."

"Yes."

"Your investment has paid off. You have over two million dollars in the parking account. I can meet you halfway, the two of us can make our investors satisfied. Thus, bringing calm to this unfortunate turn of events."

"But—"

Davies interrupted, "A temporary loan. No. A new investment. We are going bigger than the parking lots. You want to diversify, my boy. Think of how much you earned, so quickly, in the parking business. With only a little money down. Imagine what we can do with two million down."

"I'm listening."

"We can make the bad press go away with this investment. We'll use your account so nothing untoward will appear on my behalf. Put this minor trouble behind us, I can stay in the race."

Dan was intrigued. He agreed to the plan.

"One more thing, Dan. I need you to resign from

the firm. Gadly is dead to me. I will hire you and pay you in advance of your future earnings from our new venture. I will double what Gadly was paying you. I just need a little time."

"Thank you, sir. I don't know what to say."

"Make your resignation known immediately. We have a lot of work to do. Now let's meet the new bank manager and conduct our business."

The two were ushered into a room to complete the transaction. Davies saved his hide for now. He had the money to remove the target from his back. What he didn't know was this was only a reprieve. Anna, Reg, and Mayor Binks were aware of what was happening inside the bank's walls. They were concerned Dan Benchman's involvement would complicate things. Anna said Dan wouldn't be a problem.

Back at the apartment, Maggie filled Liam in on what happened at the office. They decided she should quit her job. Liam's book money and the advance from the TV studio set them up for now. They talked about moving to London, to be near Jack and Abam, far away from Nashville.

Maggie talked about starting a PR firm, avoiding Gadly's con artists. She wanted a business that wouldn't set her moral code on fire. Ideals are blueprints. Maggie's design would have a floor of ethics banning people like George Davies. Something closer to decency.

Maggie began drafting her resignation letter. She

planned on a month's notice to help with the transition. She revised her letter several times. The initial version was long-winded. Too personal. She deleted it and wrote another. Too grateful. She decided on a terse, professional note. She'd present it to Gadly in the morning.

In the next room, Liam planned to propose to Maggie this weekend. He thought he might be rushing things but something inside him felt like he needed to rush. He'd ask Maggie after dinner as they walked about the city. Maggie loved walking around Nashville at night. Near the river, under the lights of the Nashville skyline. He could see a way out.

Liam made reservations for Friday evening. He thought to check the weather. All looked clear.

What would married life look like? A quaint place in London. Maggie's workspace, styled French. France in London. Walk for coffee in the morning and again in the afternoon. They'd laugh acting like tourists in their new home—poking fun at themselves for how much they enjoyed the tour of Buckingham Palace. Listening to The Smiths, Maggie would prod Liam about Morrissey's peculiar nationalism. Liam said Moz had banked points for quoting George Eliot—a woman writing under a man's name to avoid stereotypes. The expectation of women writing light fare, as she called it.

A lot of people get weird ideas when they grow old. Liam chalked it up to Morissey's general fussiness. Then he'd catch her singing a lyric about knowing how

Joan of Arc felt.

At the weekends, they'd shop in the local markets, finding cheap little trinkets for their home. He imagined them sipping tea from an old, chipped set, wondering about the years of conversations hiding in the porcelain. They'd talk about having kids then decide to put it off for a few more years. Liam writes novels; Maggie runs her PR company. Dinners with Jack and Abam. The two couples taking turns hosting parties in their London flats. When Jack slipped into a faux British accent, Abam would remind him how ridiculous he sounded.

Simple afternoons like walking through a grocery store or having a technician over to upgrade the internet service. In this future timeline, Maggie grew potted flowers in the window, and every few years, Liam repainted the rooms. They'd order a new bedroom set, and Maggie would become hysterical watching Liam attempt to put the bed set together while navigating the cramped London space. At the end of the night, she'd kick off her shoes, relax on the sofa with a glass of wine, her long legs over his lap. He'd rub her bare feet as they talked, playing with her painted toenails. Maggie's skin was soft, undisturbed by the stress of recent events. They'd fall asleep watching a movie.

She couldn't imagine life without him. And he, without her.

***

With Davies determined to stay in the race, Mayor Binks and Reg decided it was time to act. Davies survived the plot against him. Anna knew there was only one way forward. They planned to use Dan Benchman as bait to trap then kill George Davies. Dan would also be murdered and buried alongside his mentor—probably in a junkyard. The new plan involved using Gadly's office, a place they knew well. It sat on a quiet street. A meeting would be arranged after business hours, assuring the conspirators there'd be as few people as possible on the block.

Now that Davies had cut ties with Gadly, the mayor would propose a new opportunity, one benefiting both Binks and Gadly. The Binks scandal was old news. He knew Gadly needed a high-level client to replace Davies. The first order of business would be to convince Davies to drop out of the race. They'd invite him to the meeting with an offering in return for his quitting. Davies was a man with a price. He'd entertain a generous offer.

Davies knew Anna from his associations with Gus Tower and the bank. Like everyone else, he had no idea who the real Anna was. The meeting was set up. Erasing Davies would give Binks an opening to return to the mayor's office.

Reg would place his henchmen near the building should things spiral out of control. They didn't have to worry about Gadly going to the cops because Anna had overheard his conversation in a restaurant with Caitlin talking about Charlie's poisoning. Caitlin was an accomplice too. Her new lover murdered her husband. She also benefited financially from not only her husband's corrupt businesses but what she'd inherited after his death. She could speak to no one. The mayor wanted assurances that they wouldn't touch Gadly or Caitlin. Reg gave his word. Anna was silent on the matter.

The wild card was Maggie Franklin. Mayor Binks liked Maggie and didn't want her to get hurt. He also knew she was clean. She could go to the cops. They needed to be sure she wouldn't be in the office the day of the Davies meeting. Reg knew Maggie was freelancing and proposed a meeting with a bogus client to distract her from the office. Anna suggested someone in the arts. Liam would tag along, another distraction. This created space to execute the mission against the Candidate. The mayor reminded his conspirators there was little room for error. Anna interjected there must be a nuclear option should things get out of hand. If necessary, she'd silence everyone. Reg reassured Anna by confirming his men would be nearby, on-call should matters escalate.

Anna would handle the details regarding Maggie's bogus client. Mayor Binks planned to reach out to Gadly. Reg was to approach George Davies with the offer. Everything will be in place by the middle of next week. They needed to move while Davies was still feeling the heat from his recent scandal.

21

Time to Move on

Maggie knocked, Gadly invited her inside his office. She approached his desk with her notice.

"What's this?" he asked.

"I'm giving my resignation today," she said.

Gadly read the note. He frowned his brow, removed his glasses.

"I'm sorry to hear this. I'm surprised. I thought you were happy here."

"I am. I was— I started a company. A small PR thing. Company." She felt the urge to downplay her excitement and her company. The part of her brain strong enough to move on lost the border war to the people-pleaser side.

"I see. This is disappointing news. Well, disappointing for me. But it sounds good to you. You'll be missed around here. I'm sure your company will be great."

"Thank you. I'm excited. A little scared. But more excited than scared." The 'strong enough to move on' part was now making a comeback.

"A new adventure. You'll be a success. I'm sure of that."

She smiled back but wondered why tears filled her eyes. She was relieved to quit but felt sad all the same. Another chapter ending. Gadly noticed her eyes going red.

"Maggie, you'll be fine... more than fine. I want you to know if you need anything, I'm here to help."

"I appreciate that. I appreciate everything you've done for me. I've learned so much."

"According to this note, we have you for another month?"

"Yes. I want to make the transition as smooth as I can."

"Fantastic," he paused to check his email. "So, it seems we have a meeting next week with the former mayor, Binks. On Wednesday. A small team has assembled to advise George Davies to drop out of the race. We cut ties with him, but we'll assist with this endeavor. They plan to buy him out. As you know, everything with Davies is transactional. It may work."

"Next Wednesday, what time?"

"After six P.M. Everyone meets no later than six-thirty. The time is loose because, well—it's Davies. We'll do our best to get him here. I'll have Dan handle that detail."

"I'm sorry I can't attend. I have a meeting with a potential client at the same time. They are in town for the day. I'm afraid it can't be moved."

"I guess we'll have to get used to operating without you around. If anything changes, do let us know."

"I will. Thank you for understanding."

"That'll be all," he said.

She left Gadly's office and passed Caitlin in the hallway. Caitlin squeezed Maggie's shoulder as she passed without stopping. An uncomfortable smile. Maggie turned to see her enter Gadly's office without knocking. Caitlin closed the door behind her. Entering his office without knocking was out of the ordinary. Maggie sensed something unusual about work today. She couldn't explain the sensation and wondered if it had to do with her resignation. It felt like breaking up with a long-time lover. How soon something or someone so familiar becomes like a stranger.

She arrived at her desk to work through the tension. With Davies gone, she didn't have much to do. She began drafting instructions for her replacement—directions that would have been helpful when she started working for Gadly. When she arrived from Kansas City, she felt lost in the job. By making herself look busy, she created work Gadly came to adopt as a regular part of his expectations. Gadly relied on Maggie.

In the early days, Gadly was depressed, distracted, and not much help. Caitlin was distant, unapproachable. Maggie's relationship with Caitlin changed when they mingled outside of work. The red wine loosened Caitlin's nerves. She liked Maggie. That happened a year into the job.

Maggie felt sorry for the next 'Maggie.' Dan became aggressive with his drive to climb whatever ladder of success he envisioned for himself. She noticed Dan mimicking Davies. He referred to things as being a 'zero-sum game', using baseball analogies to separate camps into winners and losers. Dan Benchman from Chicago used to be kind and polite. Now his interactions were impatient ones. He raised his voice on the phone, making demands. It carried over into his personal life. Once on the phone, she overheard Dan badgering a customer service rep about his internet connection at home: "It's slower than you, you fucking dope." Sensing a stratum of power beneath him, he took the opportunity to release whatever resentments had built up inside and turned the next fifteen minutes into a verbal onslaught aimed at the minimum wage worker on the other end of the line. Everyone was an "idiot." They were all beneath contempt, in his view. His grudges piled so high he couldn't see the forest for the trees.

Even Caitlin had changed. Her sweet affections evaporated like water to steam. When they did occur, they felt compulsory. She didn't smile like she used to. At least like she'd been smiling for the past year. She and Maggie used to talk for hours about all kinds of things, but now they spoke only of work. On occasions when Maggie asked about her weekend, Caitlin responded tersely. Her single-syllable staccato was at odds with her former self, a cultured woman who philosophized romantically about long lunches in Paris.

When Maggie invited her out for drinks or a movie night — as they used to — she'd decline. Caitlin and Gadly were now inseparable. She spent more time in his office than not. They started coming to work together. Then leaving together. If he stayed late, so did she. Gadly's calendar became hers. Maggie noticed that, at meetings, Caitlin spoke on his behalf. There were times where, if one didn't know better, Caitlin sounded like the CEO. Gadly was captivated by Caitlin. For her part, she was in love with him but also enjoyed a renewed sense of power. Maggie was curious if something more was in play than the charming couple let on.

Caitlin and Gadly, a united front. This was new. Not long ago, Caitlin frequently disagreed with Gadly. Now there is no light between them. Equally troubling was it seemed like it was more than business. And if it was more than love and business, what else could be causing their unbroken solidarity? The mystery of this affair consumed her. Maggie wasn't prone to believing in ghosts, but the office now felt haunted. There was an impending sense of doom over everything. The air was thick like chimney smoke. Every conversation was tense. Client interactions were rife with potential catastrophe. Maggie was left out of important conversations. She'd grown prodigious at doing her job even though she had no idea what was really going on. The only certainty was she couldn't wait to leave. It felt cursed in every way. It wasn't the impulse to run from problems; instead, it was survival. An instinct pushed

Maggie to the exit. There was something dangerous here. Now she regretted giving Gadly thirty days' notice. One month seemed too long—dangerously long. But she gave her word and felt stuck. Maggie was scared. Her allies had deserted her. The hurricane was on the way, and she didn't think she was safe. The dam won't hold.

The wheels bounced on the runway, then steadied, with Jack and Abam landing in America. Ignoring that Maggie hates surprises, Jack didn't tell Liam they were coming. From the car, Jack called. After checking into the hotel, they agreed to meet at the apartment for drinks before planning what to do that evening.

Since it was Abam's first time in Nashville, Jack was excited to show her around the city. From the airport to the hotel, she noticed a billboard on the highway that read: JESUS SAVES. She thought it says too much and not enough at the same time.

The other images catching her attention were the frequent pro-gun bumper stickers on trucks passing by on the road. It reminded her of imagery associated with Boko Haram back in Nigeria. Boko Haram means "Western education is forbidden." How backwards this all seemed in a so-called advanced nation. The landscape changed as they entered the city's center. She noticed a few Black Lives Matter signs and a billboard promoting an upcoming Frida Kahlo exhibit at the Frist Art Museum. The South seemed to have a kind of whiplash to it. Something she hadn't experienced in New York or London.

They reached the hotel. The concierge welcomed them, assisting with their bags. Jack kissed Abam. He kissed her as she tilted her head to feel the weight of his lips on her neck. They lived in the phase of their relationship where they could peel each other naked at any time.

Jack grew up in a Midwest bubble. Abam was a woman of the world. She spoke multiple languages while the best he could muster was counting to ten in two. Abam was philosophical. Quoted poetry at length or plucked sonnets by heart. Abam learned to read early. She first came to see the outside world — the broader world from Gusau, Zamfara's capital — through books. She dreamed of living in London one day, and that's what she did.

Abam spent the wet season — summer — playing along the Sokoto River with her friends and cousins. They watched the rain and its choreographed dance, graceful splashes on top of the water. It sounded like an ensemble's rumbling fingertips on a desktop.

When the rain stopped, Abam would stare at the tops of her feet, appearing then disappearing on the bank's edge, in mud and cloudy brown water; washed clean through the tiny borders of her toes. As a teenager, the dam collapsed and destroyed her family home. Her memories of the river are a combination of joy and devastation mixed up like sand.

She spoke to Jack about the tyranny of things, material things. Abam gorged on ideas and experiences. Though fashionable, she was incorruptible by competition. She saw value in creating. Value in telling stories, stories of those without a voice, or suppressed voices. These were gifts passed down by her mother and grandmother. Life wisdom. Not learned but lived.

Abam spent afternoons sneaking into the local school's library. There she made friends with the librarian, who suggested books she should read. She read beyond her years. Once, as a birthday gift, the librarian gave her a copy of the sonnets. Apart from a small suitcase with her clothes, it's the only thing she took with her when she left Africa. It survived the flood.

It's like the river wanted her to leave. Destroying her home relieved her of the guilt of leaving *home*. Nothing left to regret. Her mother wanted Abam to know the smell and feel of a different place. Abam lost her house at age thirteen. She left Nigeria at age seventeen.

A relative gave Abam the opportunity to study in New York. The swollen river carved a path.

Jack got his start in acting by playing Marcus Antonius, which created poetry, symmetry — in Abam's mind — to their meeting. It was Shakespeare that brought together a Midwest boy and a Nigerian girl to meet in a city like London. What she couldn't have foreseen was how *Julius Caesar* was soon to rhyme with their lives.

***

193

The two couples were hanging out on the rooftop of Liam and Maggie's building. Jack and Liam talked about the show. Abam joked about her struggle to arrange furniture in a tiny London flat. Maggie told everyone she had given Gadly her notice. She spoke with nervous energy about striking out on her own. Abam held Maggie's hand and gave a list of reasons why she'd be successful. Abam challenged Maggie to embrace uncertainty. This made Maggie nervous.

Abam and Jack committed to helping Maggie. Abam leased a workspace in London with room available. Liam and Maggie planned to look for a flat. They discussed which possessions they'd sell and how much they'd ship overseas. Maggie had heirlooms she'd take with her, but aside from a few pieces, they were content to travel light, start anew.

The conversation turned dark as Maggie spoke about George Davies and all that was happening at work. She, again, voiced concern about his involvement in the TV show. Jack said Davies was investing indirectly through one of his associates. His colleague had invested in the tech company which housed the movie studio. Jack said productions of this size found investors from a wide range of people. It was impossible to know what portion of the money, if any, was clean or exactly how much was generated from corrupt sources like Davies. Not everyone in the pharmaceutical industry is a criminal. The job of sniffing out corruption is so massive it's paralyzing. Jack can't solve that puzzle. Maggie agreed with much of what he said but argued that Davies has a way of ruining what he touches. Bloated, greedy cancer. Jack promised her Davies couldn't hurt the show. Maggie told him it wasn't the show that kept her awake at night.

Liam's plan to propose to Maggie was now interrupted by the surprise visit. He snuck away to change the reservation to a table of four. The others left the rooftop to refill drinks.

Back inside the apartment, Jack was under attack from a sneezing fit he couldn't stop. Liam had surprised Maggie — Surprise! — with a kitten, a gray tabby named Leo. He attached himself to Jack. Jack was now learning of his cat allergy, but Leo was so adorable he couldn't keep from giving the sweet little guy a chin scratch. Liam returned to find Jack's condition getting worse. To alleviate Jack's itchy eyes, the couples parted ways to get dressed for the night with plans to meet later at the restaurant Liam had booked.

Back in their hotel room, while Jack zipped up Abam's dress, she asked if he was sure Davies was harmless. He gave her the same speech he'd given Maggie. Jack kissed the nape of her neck. Another version of: Everything will be fine. Promise.

He explained, "Davies is a tiny player in a game he doesn't understand. Guys like him want the glamour of television. Davies bought his way into the party. The studio execs will introduce him to a few famous people, Davies will be impressed with himself, and that'll be the end of it. It's like paying to rent an exotic car for the afternoon."

Abam smiled in return as if to say she felt good about the arrangement. In her heart, she remained worried. There was something about the way Maggie spoke of George Davies. She sensed a storm though she couldn't place it exactly. She worked hard to convince herself all was well because that's the outcome she hoped for. We sometimes lie to ourselves to bend the universe in our direction. Abam is wise, but even she's not immune to this deficiency in the human condition.

Inside the dimly lit restaurant, the couples laughed at the accidental choreography of their dark clothes. The girls wore black dresses and heels. The men dressed in slim black suits like they were attending a stylish funeral. Some gallows humor ensued about this being the last time the four of them would dine together. They raised glasses to one final night out. A toast of prescience.

Over dinner, Jack mentioned that his father's health was deteriorating. He and Abam planned to visit his parents so they could meet her in person. Unfortunately, Amis was dying from Alzheimer's. Jack's mother was having trouble caring for him. The family made plans for Amis to move to a long-term care facility. Living in another country now, Jack thought this trip could be the last time he'd see his father alive.

Rita said Amis still played guitar. His peace. A salve for anger and frustration. He forgot people's names. Unaware of the disease, stealing his mind.

Rita wanted Amis to play. His fingers paused the disease, with guitar. With jazz. To the music, Rita danced like she was still in his arms, blissfully unaware of their current predicament. His playing, beautiful like Rita. Amis hummed along while his fingers found the notes.

Eyes closed, head cocked, she imagined walking by his side in New York on a snowy day. Inside this daydream, Amis put his arm around Rita, bracing her from the cold. She listened while he talked about the great jazz musicians, walking the same streets. He told her about Freddie Keppard bringing the sound of New Orleans to New York.

He said, "Close your eyes. Imagine standing on the corner of Fifth Avenue and 42nd Street in the 1920s."

New York in the 1920s was the sound of his playing. Jack thought his father could have been a famous musician. But jazz doesn't make the same money as popular music. Amis wouldn't chase a music career that required trading taste for money. So, he saved music for himself like a sacred prayer uncorrupted by the business of making music. Amis had practical concerns. He had a family to support so he discovered other ways to sustain himself.

Rita loved Amis; they had always remained close. Both were proud of their son. After success, Jack flew them to movie premieres. Amis and Rita loved the experience. Jack was grateful for their encouragement. He didn't know how much he needed it. Jack lied to himself about his self-esteem issues. When it boiled in his body, he changed the subject. A new girl. A new gig. More compliments. Money. These things helped keep the pirates at bay.

Rita helped Jack prepare for his first role playing Mark Antony in his high school's production of *Julius Caesar*. She read with him for hours, inspiring her son to look deeper, get inside the characters. Rita taught Jack not what to think but how to think.

Jack was heartbroken. Helpless against the disease killing his dad. For a man to lose his mind is a cruel fate—nature's indifference to human affairs. A conscious universe wouldn't be so malevolent. But Amis played on, Rita danced, and that is how they found poise. But Jack had to confront the dark moments of a dying parent.

Amis was sick beyond Rita's ability to care for him. He needed professional help. She'd visit him every day; they'd dine together. Amis loved to play chess. The game hadn't escaped his memory. Chess and jazz. Rita held to them like a religion. A faded glimpse into the way things used to be. For now, she couldn't bear it any other way. Soon she'd have no choice.

Maggie's parents were still independent, but they were getting older. She tried letting go of the grudges. Tried to let the past live where it lives. Maggie had learned to cope with her father's anger. Her mother's absence. She needed to see them as they knew they would never live up to what she wished they'd be. Maggie rationalized that her parents did their best but fell short, like everyone. She knew they loved her but felt conflicted by the pain they caused. Scar tissue. Emotional scars. Maggie's father only hit her a few times. Only.

What's the statute of limitations on heartbreak? It seems cruel to dig up old offenses against aging parents. They become like children—weak, feeble. Too little. Too late. A lost cause.

Maggie couldn't let it go. Would she be repeating the same behavior?

Scolding a mother and father like children. It seemed insufferable or, at least, inappropriate. They were closer to the end of their lives. What would that say about Maggie? Is she willing to volley sorrow and guilt at her parents for making her feel this way in the first place? Sorrow, a kind of palsy gripping the family as it grows into resentment like an untamed forest. Guilt begs the question, what can we do about this now?

Maggie is twenty-eight. Her parents were in their forties when she was born. An accidental pregnancy. I was an accident, she thought. Her sister wasn't.

As always, Maggie chose to harbor the pain to shield others from the anguish of guilt.

Liam's relationship with his parents was complicated too. Conflicted even further after his father died. His mother didn't see writing as a real job, though it was she who introduced him to books.

She drove Liam to the public library. After a few hours of browsing, they'd head home with a stack of books full of the stories that filled his imagination. She read to him at bedtime. After they finished a book, she'd ask questions to be sure he paid attention. Liam's mother was impressed by the details he absorbed, even pointing her to parts of the story she'd missed. Liam noticed when her mind was drifting while she read. Her voice would leave the character impressions, replaced instead with a monotonous plateau. He'd tug on her shirt to reel her in, back inside the thick plot where she'd find her voice. Liam clung to those impressions, her voices, as he imagined himself being the protagonist. He lived chapter to chapter, eager for the plot to reveal itself. It was then that he learned to write. Put another way: it was how he learned to tell stories. And his mother planted those seeds. She gave him the thing she tried to take away.

Jack held the opposite view of his parents. But he felt guilty living far away from them while his father was dying. With his mother left behind, catching the pieces of a once whole family.

Maggie spent her young life chasing away the ghosts of her past. The Sisyphean task of ignoring her father's voice — a man without reason — as she struggled with insecurity. She avoided the temptations of her mother's impulse to check out. Her life would be different from theirs. Liam is not her father. Thank God for that.

As they traded childhood stories, the impulse for self-pity changed with the subject of things about their parents they cherished. The waitstaff was polite and professional, but their table outgrew its welcome. Closing time had come and gone. The waitstaff tactfully urged the group out of the building. They began strolling east toward the river. Jack and Abam held hands under the clear sky as Maggie fell into the security of Liam's arms. They walked a few blocks before reaching the hotel. Hugging and saying their goodbyes, Jack surprised Liam by telling him he loved him. Not that Liam doubted their friendship, it's just not something they said to each other.

Liam said, "I love you too."

Abam invited them in for one more drink at the bar. Maggie declined, and the couples parted ways a little before midnight.

Liam looked up as the stars blinked down on them. How lucky they were to be alive.

"I know things have been chaotic. But it's getting better, right? I feel like we are pulling out of a long storm."

"It does feel that way. It feels good," she said.

Liam stopped by a small green area. He guided Maggie to a bench under a streetlamp. It wasn't chilly outside, but Maggie felt the light's warmth as Liam sat next to her.

He said, "When I came back from New York, my life felt wasted. The high of being in New York was gone. I was *back* at home. Going *back*wards. In New York I was somewhere. In KC, my parents were right. I wasn't going to be a writer. I was done. I was back, back, back."

"Liam, stop."

"Let me finish. The summer after college, I was aimless. Looking for something new but dragging through the past. Like a kindness, you stopped me in my tracks. My life changed. It became defined by: Before Maggie, After Maggie—B.M., A.M."

They giggled as Maggie blushed, looking down at her toes, visible as she removed her heels, freeing her feet for the evening breeze. She crossed her legs then looked up again at Liam.

He said, "On our first night together, I felt like I was floating. I could trust you. I could tell you anything."

Liam had spent his life chasing perfection, knowing that it was impossible. But he kept coming back to that word with Maggie. On a knee in the middle of the crowded park... Liam paused for breath. His heart was doing its best to get out. Nervous lips.

Maggie's cheeks flushed. She didn't care about the crowd of strangers gathering around them. She was smiling. Wiping away tears was pointless. Liam fumbled for the box in his pocket, turning the fabric of his jacket inside out; took her hand, put the ring on her finger, and asked Maggie to marry him. She answered: "Yes." Echoed through more tears. They hugged and kissed to the standing applause of strangers under the July stars. Liam helped Maggie up to stand with him on the park bench. They bowed as if they'd wrapped a scene on a stage. Liam, now mucking it up with the audience, removed his jacket, placed it over her shoulders, and took his fiancée home.

22

What's Become of Us?

Michael reached his limit with Dan's new persona as his partner became someone he didn't recognize. Though the history between them isn't long, Dan had abandoned the traits that attracted Michael in the first place. They crossed paths in Chicago, introduced to one another by a mutual friend who, as it happens, was a police officer. Michael had come out to his family. It wasn't going well. His family was religious, and the news of a gay son wasn't welcome. Michael, two years older than Dan, took a job at a community college teaching photography. Dan was finishing a degree at the University of Chicago.

After an awkward introduction by their friend, Dan and Michael bonded. In their old life they'd see bands at The Metro, go to the movies, watch the Cubs. Michael wasn't at all interested in sports, but Dan's knowledge of baseball enamored him. He listened as Dan talked about the history of the game. The history of Wrigley Field. After the Cubs won the World Series, Dan couldn't work for a week. Michael edited photos even as the deciding game went to extra innings. Dan found Michael's contrarian lack of interest in sports attractive.

They gave each other new experiences. Michael devoured his first hot dog at the ballpark. He dragged Dan to art galleries. Dan didn't understand art installations any more than Michael understood what the hell a balk was or why the umps took issue with the move. Dan looked older than his age. Michael wondered if Dan was pretending to be younger out of vanity or because he was embarrassed about still being a student. He'd jab his partner about his mysteriousness, joking that Dan was a secret agent. The couple laughed it off as they dressed for a night out in Wicker Park.

They weren't dating long when Dan decided to move to Nashville, where his father secured a job for him at Gadly's PR agency. He wasn't excited about the offer but preferred it to working for his old man, whom he resented. Dan and Michael never met each other's families—not much known about each other's past. Their unknown histories didn't matter. They reinvented together. Dan was no longer a failed, injured baseball player. Michael was no longer Mike.

Dan gave Michael an excuse to quit his family, or at least an excuse to distance himself from his family. Michael helped Dan move past his father's overbearing influence.

"Aren't you grateful your father helped you land a job?" Michael asked.

"I'm thankful he's taking the cuffs off."

"Your father sounds like an asshole, but some assholes see the sun."

"Whatever. Are you nervous about moving?"

"In a way. I'm happy to put a few states between me and my family. But I gave up a good teaching gig at the college. I'm nervous to start over in a new city. I hope I can find work."

"I have a rich dad; he's good for something. We'll be fine. I can support you until you're on your feet."

Michael was uneasy about the arrangement. Dan had an obsessive personality. He was controlling. They'd be in a new city, knowing almost no one, and he was now relying on Dan to pay the bills. He felt the pressure to find work fast. Michael was suffocating from the stress of the situation. In Nashville, Dan bought a house leaving Michael's name off the deed and out of every decision. Anchored by insecurities from childhood, he didn't have the voice to stand his ground against Dan. Dan knew this and didn't waste the advantage he held over his partner. Michael wasn't sure if Dan loved him or if he loved the power imbalance.

Their paths now seemed divergent. Michael wanted to move out west to pursue photography. Dan was obsessed not only with work but with wealth. They only went out if there was an opportunity to advance Dan's career. Owing to the obsession, Dan was always stressed; most conversations between the two ended in angry debates. Dan had the habit of finding an argument on every topic. He argued about things he knew nothing about. Loud and confident without a shred of expertise. Money was a trigger. First, the home renovation was too expensive. Then the remodel wasn't impressive enough. They needed to get bigger. Dan pressured Michael to invest. With his savings dwindling, Michael was scared to put money into Dan's business with George Davies.

Dan earned decent money working for Gadly and with his father's fortune, he could help Michael cover his bills. The downside was, he then held this over Michael's head like bizarre collateral. Dan's cruelty bloomed with power. If Dan's goal was to push Michael away, he succeeded.

One day, after a round of verbal abuse, Michael walked out. While Dan was at the office, Michael ordered a moving truck. Headed west alone. He left a short note explaining his unhappiness, and the two never spoke again. He told Dan not to worry about repaying his share of the investment. Michael didn't care about the money. It was a small price to pay for his freedom.

Dan didn't mention the breakup to anyone. Not even George Davies. He had become so focused on his work he was numb to emotions. To relationships. He felt nothing over Michael's exit. Alone, in a large, empty house, Dan was surprised to find he was contented with loneliness. There was no sadness, no regret. Nothing.

What had become of him? In navigating the world

of George Davies, Dan created a character to play. He became the man he invented. He erased the space between the man he once was and who he is now. The breaking point from falsetto to chest voice was undetectable. It's like the evolution of a child. You don't at once see a toddler become a teen. It's a gradual evolution where the changes are noticeable only in hindsight. That's what's become of Dan Benchman, a former star pitcher. He once leaned on the wise words of his grandfather. Now his sage is George Davies. Dan was drunk with ambition and hungry for power. He could feel his humanity leaving him. Everything was transactional. He treated people as chess pieces to be expertly removed from the board. The bitterness over who he'd become only hardened his lust. Dan was lost and knew there was nothing, no one who could stop him. Adrift from the things that make us human, Dan embraced the darkness as a mechanism for self-defense. He couldn't be hurt if he could no longer feel. And because he no longer felt anything, he was prepared to punish at will.

23

Going Home to Say Goodbye

Rita prepared lunch for the special guests, excited to host her daughter-in-law, whom she'd only spoken with over the phone. Amis was in the study, unaware of the purpose of this visit. He was unaware of the visit itself. He remembered his son but didn't know who Abam was or why she was standing in front of him. Jack introduced his wife. Amis scolded Jack for not inviting his parents to the wedding. Abam spoke in a gentle way that made Amis smile. As the day wore on, he wouldn't remember Abam as his son's wife, but her calming voice was welcome anyway.

Jack told his parents about life in London. He took them on a virtual tour of their flat and spoke with enthusiasm about his favorite places. Jack reminisced about the music scene and said someday Amis should fly to London to experience it himself. Impossible because of his condition, but the joy it brought Amis in the meantime was nice.

Rita shared a family recipe with Abam. It was an old Yorkshire pudding recipe inherited from her father's side of the family. They laughed at how unhealthy and delicious it was. Rita had prepared the dish for their visit. She gave Abam a sneak taste. Abam was in love with the pudding, and Rita, in love with her daughter-in-law. They bonded over identity. The identities of birth. Identities of experience. Rita's father was British, white. Her mother, Black. Abam spoke of adjusting from Nigeria to the United States. Then again in Britain. Rita grew up asking: Who am I? Where do I belong? As life unfolded for them, the answers to those questions were revealed, sometimes mutating into something surprising. What became obvious was they now felt like family.

Jack was an only child, although they had tried for others. Rita suffered two miscarriages. After years of trying, Rita and Amis stopped grasping for what they didn't have. They held Jack even tighter.

Jack admired Amis, the way he dedicated himself to his craft—jazz guitar. Amis inspired Jack to take acting seriously. "If you're going to do something, *do it*." he said.

When Jack was a young boy, Amis put on old records. Talked about the greats. Jack was drawn to the Blue Note album jackets—Reid Miles artwork and Bauhaus. Jack then studied actors from earlier generations. He scoured every genre of film. Jack watched foreign films with the subtitles off, studying faces and actions. He didn't understand the language, so it was like a story without words. Like his father's instrumentals.

Jack skipped college. He had his teachers. Amis and the greats.

Rita was teasing them about kids—eager for grandchildren. Abam blushed and smiled. Jack said it would be a while. They loved their lives. Had big plans.

"Mom, how can I chase my dreams if I'm busy chasing kids?"

"You'd be surprised. You adapt when the little ones come along,"

Abam joined in. "Jack would have to spend less time in front of the mirror."

"Betrayed."

They laughed. Normal returned but it wouldn't stay.

After dinner, Amis reached for his guitar, plugged in. Abam, with a velvet voice, hummed along. Amis put the chords beneath her singing, supporting then surrounded her with a dusty old Gibson 355, adrift in reverb. Jack and Rita danced. Amis closed his eyes, smiled a broad smile. Rita missed this. The music played for hours. Amis milked each tone as he wandered from one chord to the next. Abam was in sync with his playing as they bent musical time, unbound by the limitations of meter, making bar lines disappear like the strokes on a painting the farther away you step. Rita wanted to bottle the moment. She knew how fleeting it was but remained thankful for the night's specialness regardless of the ephemeral nature of it all. Her family was together. She brought out her vintage Canon 35mm camera. They took turns taking pictures. The neat thing about this camera was how it stretched the experience. A lingering surprise was waiting, developing the memories days or weeks later.

Jack and Abam took turns picking records. Amis had an old console turntable. Perfectly warm and scratchy. It still looked new. Discovering old records for the first time is new for the listener. A treasure hunt not dissimilar to the improvisations of a jazz musician.

The Yorkshire pudding arrived at the table. Amis and Jack helped themselves for seconds. With a lively conversation all around him, Amis fell asleep in his leather chair.

Rita later woke Amis and guided him to the bedroom. She dressed him for bed, propping his tired feet. Asleep, he drifted. She stared at his bare feet. Soft on top while the bottoms archived a lifetime of walking and working.

Rita thought back to those feet standing at the end of the aisle on their wedding day. She remembered how strong his feet were the day he helped her to the hospital—the day Jack was born. Feet that carried a family, walking and working. A little boy running, jumping. A young man in love, dancing. The old man, dying. Rita fought back tears while Amis slept. The door closed behind her as she left the room. She joined Jack and Abam on the couch, and they discussed what to do with Amis.

Rita had secured an assisted living facility not too

far from home. She wanted Amis close. Not to shorten her commute. Rita wanted Amis to feel as close to home as possible.

Amis's condition had reached a point beyond her care. Due to Jack's successful career, cost wasn't an issue. Amis would spend the final chapter of his life with dignity. They would try music therapy. Music seemed to be the one thing to slow dementia.

Jack couldn't speak about Amis without swollen eyes. Rita was strong. She said it will be a series of steps. One foot. Then the next. In her private moments, she was overwhelmed by the reality of losing her husband. Overwhelmed by helping her husband with death. What is especially cruel about this disease is the way it removes the mind from the body. It leaves its victims with a still-functioning body, but one that no longer remembers their spouse or child.

Rita still saw the same young man she fell in love with years ago. The handsome man who took her to speakeasies. The man who'd surprise her with flowers without occasion.

"What's all this fuss for?" she asked.

"You love flowers."

"You know we don't have the extra money."

"Don't talk about money right now. Let's dance."

Amis held her in his arms and led Rita around the dining room. If a record wasn't spinning on the console, he'd sing something in its place while they danced. Now was not the time to spare pennies. Let go. Enjoy life.

Amis taught Rita to let go. She taught him to be thrifty. Some lessons he ignored.

A wonderful marriage. Before Jack was born, they'd go out late. Going out at bedtime. Dinner and drinks with friends. Late nights dancing followed by an even later night inviting everyone to their home for Amis's impromptu jams. He'd reach for the Gibson, an ES-175—Sunburst, or 355—Cherry. Amis wasn't thrifty.

Friends pulled records from the shelf. With the mind of a library, Amis recalled every lick. He named the artist, year of recording, composer, etc. A real-time musicologist. His passion for music spilled over into his passion for life. It may not need to be said, but Amis loved living.

A proud papa. When Jack's career exploded, Amis searched the public library for books on acting. He wanted to know his son's language. While Jack lived in Los Angeles, he'd call to talk about what he'd read about Charlie Chaplin. Amis connected silent movies to instrumental music. Pictures without sound. Sound without words. Interpretation without explanation.

Amis explained how a great musician could say so much with only a few notes. Jack hung on to this advice. While filming, he earned a reputation on the set for editing lines. This sent writers and directors into a panic. Jack improvised on the set too. Another gift from Amis. Composing in real time like a jazz musician. A jazz performance is the search for discovery. Jack saw acting in the same light. Discovery.

Jack understood the storytelling. He took from movies as he borrowed from music. These two things taught him pace. Timing. Beats. It was all the same to him. These lessons were gifts from Amis. A lifetime of wisdom passed from a father to a child, now shared with strangers around the world watching his films.

His father never became a world-renowned musician. A book won't be written about Amis Howe (apart from this one). His life's work lives on in Jack. A continuation. It's as close to immortality as you get. Jack held this gift like a rare heirloom. One day, when he and Abam start a family, Jack will pass it on to their children. Amis endures despite his failing mind. What a beautiful life.

Amis lived another year in the care facility. He became more agitated as his mind gave in to the disease. The good days were rare. He made friends with the nursing staff, who all enjoyed hearing him play guitar. Rita visited but dreaded when it was time to leave. Amis was loud. Angry when visiting hours were over. He didn't understand why she was leaving him behind in this damn building. Why couldn't he come home with her? He wanted to sleep in *his* bed. She held firm in front of Amis, but when Rita sat in her car in the parking lot, she sobbed like a child. Driving home alone, she'd see others on the sidewalk, talking and laughing with their loved ones. She felt the sounds of life leaving her ears.

Rita was entering her own silent movie, but she was going on alone, against her will.

The house was as quiet as death when Rita walked through the front door. She placed the keys in a brass tray on the counter. There were days when she didn't have the energy to hang her coat in the closet, so, on those days, she'd lay it over the back of a dining chair. Other days, it was abandoned on the couch. On her worst days, she'd drop her coat and purse in the entryway. Walk straight to the bedroom. Rita slept for hours, or she'd lie awake with her eyes closed. The time awake seemed like hours passed when only fifteen or twenty minutes had expired. Hours escaped without a word, so she began talking to herself out loud because she feared losing the skill for conversation. She'd call her son, but he was busy. Rita felt guilty keeping him on the phone. Once a week, she and Abam would have lengthy phone conversations. Early morning on Saturday for Rita, early afternoon for Abam. These talks were the highlight of her week. Rita busied herself Monday through Friday to get to the weekend for their next chat.

Her new normal, a widow, came upon her like a slow car crash. Jack read somewhere that the root word of widow means "be empty." He didn't know if that was true, but it seemed right. Amis was full of life, with Rita and Jack. A family. Full. Now he was gone. Be empty.

Before Amis passed, Jack and Abam arrived in town one final time to say goodbye. Amis couldn't remember who they were. It was painful. Though they weren't religious, they chose a traditional Mass and burial. His friends and co-workers shared anecdotes. Then a small gathering at the house. Then it was over. He was really gone.

The commotion of funeral arrangements came and went. When you're planning a funeral, it feels like the person is still there. Present tense. He looks good in blue, they say. So and so will be laid to rest here. Soft language for a hard reality.

Rita had gotten used to coming home to a quiet house. But when Amis was still alive, at the care facility, things were still buoyant. After he died, the silence was thick, and it made her heart feel as heavy as a stone.

Jack convinced Rita to keep the house but moved in with him and Abam in London. The experience of living in another country was a way for Rita to steady her feet. One foot. Then the next. Jack didn't want his mom, sitting alone in an empty house, waiting to die of sadness. Learning to live in a new city gave Rita a focus point. A guide away from misery, solitude.

She brought one of his guitars to London, the red one. Hung it in the living room. Abam had commissioned an artist friend in Paris to paint Rita and Amis's wedding photo onto canvas. It sat next to the Gibson. Each day Rita spent a moment in front of the painting, where she listened for the sound of his voice. She imagined: "I love you, darling," coming from some other realm she hoped was there.

One afternoon, Jack approached his mother as she stared at the painting, lost in her thoughts. She saw Amis in Jack's face.

"Mom, do you remember the first time we traveled to New Orleans with Dad? I think I was nine, maybe ten."

"I do. You were ten. But it wasn't our first time in New Orleans with you. We visited with you as a baby."

"I always felt at home there."

"Truth be told, I became pregnant in New Orleans."

"Maybe that's why I feel at home in the French Quarter."

Rita, laughing, "No. It's the drinks and pretty girls."

"And the music."

"The food. Your father loved Cajun food. But he couldn't handle the spices. He felt invincible when he was in New Orleans. Always ordering things with extra spice."

"Make it hot."

"That's what he'd say." They laughed and it struck Jack that that's how he ordered his curry dishes.

When Maggie visited, they'd sit around the dining table and listen as Rita told stories from her youth. Before she met Amis. Jack had a hard time imagining his mom not being his mom. Before she was Rita Howe. Abam reminded Jack that, as shocking as it may be, women aren't defined by the men in their lives.

The story has moved a year forward. Now it's time to return to the present day.

24

The Cursed Encounter

It was early morning; Maggie was pacing the kitchen. She made a pot of coffee but forgot to pour it into her cup before it turned cold. Liam walked in much later in the morning, filled his mug, took a sip, recoiled with a grunt, not expecting stale coffee on his lips. He emptied the pot down the sink, brewed another. Maggie's thoughts were somewhere else.

"Are you okay?"

"I'm fine. I'm just nervous about my meeting. What if it doesn't go well?"

"She'll love you. Just be you."

She was feeling the pressure of quitting her job. Launching a new company made her sick with anxiety. Her job at Gadly's firm provided the security of a regular paycheck—though sometimes it wouldn't arrive when Caitlin was distracted.

Liam tried to calm her nerves. "Let me come with you."

"Really?"

"Really. If there's an awkward break in the conversation, I'll fill it."

"That sounds dangerous."

He made her laugh, for a moment she relaxed. He poured fresh coffee into their mugs. Her mug was more like a bowl. It was an oversized coffee cup he bought for her while in New York. Some mornings, she'd complain about the rush of caffeine making her hands shake.

"I've only had two cups today. Why am I feeling like this?"

"Two bowls."

"What?"

"Two bowls equals four cups of coffee."

"I don't think it's the coffee."

"Four cups are a lot."

"But I've only had two cups."

He quit the argument, knowing he didn't wish to die on this hill.

She opened her laptop, buried her face in the blue glow, and typed notes for the meeting. Liam left the room to shower. He came back to ask a question.

"Should I shave?"

"No. Why?"

"For the meeting. It's a new client."

"No. I like you scruffy."

"I look scruffy?"

"Leave the whiskers. I think you're handsome."

Liam checked his face in the hall mirror. He was pleased and decided not to shave.

A notification interrupted Maggie's work. The

meeting was pushed back an hour. This gave her time to go to the office to assist Gadly with Davies. Then she'll skip out early to meet her new client a block away. She didn't bother messaging him about it. He'd be pleased to have her around. Still in her robe, Maggie was relieved to have a little more time. She surprised Liam in the shower.

They dressed and went out for lunch. Over ginger ale and salad, they talked. Maggie felt light. This was her time and barely touched her food as she anticipated the future. Liam was happy to see her so optimistic.

Maggie thought back to her time in Kansas City, at the ad agency. A lifetime away from here. That job introduced her to Liam, and Gadly. Now she was starting a company. Soon, planning a wedding. They'd leave Nashville for London. She felt the rush of happiness. Maggie was calm.

She felt an extra boost of confidence. Maybe it was the sex. Maybe it was knowing she'd soon be leaving Gadly. Caffeine and life jitters gone. After lunch, she ordered a cup of coffee to go. They agreed to meet later at the office. Liam scheduled a conference call with Jack and the TV executives, so he'd be tied up until then. They kissed goodbye and walked in opposite directions.

Hours later, at the office.

"Maggie, I didn't expect you today," Caitlin said.

"My meeting was rescheduled so I thought I'd drop in to help with Davies."

"We can use your help, dear. You know how things get when he's around."

"I do. How is Gadly?"

"He's good. A little stressed but good. He wants George Davies out of his hair."

"Do you think he'll quit the race?"

"I think he has a price. The controversy has been a lot for him. My feeling is he'll take the offer and run. He wants the title, Mayor Davies, but has little interest in the job."

"What are they offering him?"

"Board membership on a public transit project. It's a job without responsibilities. He'll have a title and a paycheck as a consultant. Though, there won't be any consulting."

"Why must everything with him be so depraved?"

"That's who he is. But it's better to have him there than being elected mayor. Our city doesn't need that."

"I thought the polls looked bad for him."

"They did. But the other candidates don't have the name recognition or funding to compete. His signs are plastered everywhere. He has the budget for non-stop TV ads."

Caitlin paused. She looked concerned.

"Pardon me, I need to see Gadly." Caitlin left for his office in a hurry. Then Dan Benchman entered the room.

"Hey."

"Hi Dan."

"Didn't expect you in," he said. His attention was on his phone.

"I'm here now."

"I heard you're leaving."

"Yes. I gave Gadly my notice. I'll be here another month."

"Sorry to see you go," he said, still staring at his phone.

"I've enjoyed my time here, but I'm excited about my new company."

"Do you have another job lined up?" He wasn't listening.

"Um, yes. I started a PR company."

"That sounds good. I hope it works out for you."

"Um, thanks."

Dan never looked up from his phone as he left the room like a zombie, on his way to meet Davies. Maggie logged in to prepare for the meeting. She still didn't understand what was needed.

Caitlin entered with Gadly.

"Maggie you're a lifesaver," he said.

"I'm here to help."

"George Davies will be accompanied today by Mayor Binks, Reginald Flint, and Anna Tomášová. Or so I've been told."

"Will the former mayor—"

Gadly cut her off. "Don't call him that. He'll lose his shit if you say former mayor. And make sure there's plenty of coffee. Check to see that the bar is stocked.

Refill what's depleted."

"Will do. I can't stay for the whole meeting, but I'll have everything prepared."

"Perfect. Caitlin will arrange for you to print the documents for presentation."

Caitlin added, "They should be in your inbox now."

"I see them. Thank you."

Gadly and Caitlin left the room. No one at the office ever replied, "You're welcome." Maggie busied herself with the tasks. She was happy to help. And even happier to have an excuse to leave without having to hang around and endure George Davies any longer than she needed to.

At six o'clock Dan returned to the office with Davies. They arrived from a nearby restaurant where Dan informed the Candidate about the offer to leave the race. Dan convinced him the offer was good.

At the restaurant, the Candidate ordered cocktails. His head, heavy from drinking, nodded along, interested in making a deal.

"You've impressed me, Benchman. I'm pleased to have you on my side. But let's not give away our hand. I'll show some reluctance to the offer. Force them to sweeten the deal. Have you resigned yet?"

"No. Soon. What else do you want?"

"Anything. Make it sweeter."

"I'll push the conversation in that direction."

"I don't want to be mayor anyway. Removing

Binks was the plan from the beginning."

"You have no interest in winning the election?"

"I don't want to lose. No one runs to lose. But for me, the election was a way to generate press. Think of it as marketing I didn't have to pay for. I used other people's money to boost my profile. Stoke divisions then sit back and collect small-dollar donations. Feed them drivel like: 'Off Our Backs. No New Tax.' Or: 'Take Back Our City.' Serve it on a grievance platter and they eat it right up. You need to make them angry. Make them think there was some magical time in the past when things were better.

"That's what you do. Make it personal. There's real power in culture war. Divide the masses into groups you can pit against each other. Let them tear each other apart like wild animals fighting for food. They don't have money for healthcare, but they'll find five dollars or fifteen dollars to donate to my campaign. Ha, ha. Convince them *the future is on the ballot.* You make that pitch well and they'll open their wallets."

Dan snuck off to the bathroom and sent a message to Gadly that Davies was pliable. He wanted them to sweeten the deal. They'd make it so Davies thought he was setting the terms of his removal. Dan worked hard to reach this level of power but something about it made him sicker than watching Davies eat.

Mayor Binks, Reg, and Anna arrived before Davies. Maggie invited them in and led them to the conference room.

"Maggie, we are pleased to see you here," said Anna.

Maggie wondered how Anna knew her name. They'd never met before today.

"You must be Anna. It's good to meet you."

The mayor intervened. "We've bragged about you, Maggie."

Maggie forced a smile. She offered them something to drink. They requested a round of water and coffee. As they were seated, Dan entered with Davies.

Gadly and Caitlin were running late. They remained upstairs in his office having a final discussion of the current situation.

Reg's henchmen were parked outside, waiting for instructions. These were the same two tough guys responsible for completing the scheme that ended in Gus Tower's hanging. Reg and Mayor Binks were wired for them to hear what was going on inside the building.

"I apologize for my tardiness," announced Gadly as he appeared with Caitlin. Gadly considered himself a dandy, but today he looked disheveled. Caitlin, as always, looked exquisite.

"Mrs Cheney, how lovely you look today," Davies said, bypassing Gadly. He used her surname to remind her she was Charlie's widow.

"Nice to see you, George," she said. Caitlin was unflappable.

"Shall we begin?" Gadly led the group with a brief

statement full of flattering remarks aimed at Davies. Sycophancy worked on him. His ego opened holes in his defenses. While Gadly made his remarks, Maggie received a text message that her meeting was canceled. Her heart sank. She felt the pull of the firm tugging at her as she was desperate to leave. Anna was pulling strings, working on her own. She needed Maggie here.

Overwhelming darkness now descended on the office. Maggie wondered how ghastly things would become. Liam was due to arrive to pick her up in a short while. She didn't bother telling him the meeting was off. Maybe she'd use his arrival to excuse herself—any excuse to leave this awful place.

"I do appreciate your attention to this matter," Davies said. "Lately, I've found myself in the most unfortunate of circumstances. These recent events, as you all well know, have complicated the election. I've been advised to step away from the race."

Davies paused for what seemed like a long time. Maggie scanned the room to see all eyes were staring in his direction. He looked at the floor, then raised his head and continued.

"Your offer is generous. I am a man of principle [He is not]. I want what's best for Nashville [He does not]. And in the interest of what is best, I will accept the fair offer before me."

As Davies continued, Liam arrived. Maggie excused herself to greet him at the front door. She told him to wait in the lobby. She'd remove herself from the meeting as soon as she could. He helped himself to coffee. Maggie returned to the conference room. Everyone was tense with friction. Liam was flipping through a copy of the *New Yorker* when he was interrupted by a knock at the door. Reg's henchmen entered. Liam unwittingly guided them to the meeting room.

Mayor Binks rose to speak. "George, you ruined my career, my marriage, my reputation. Your scheme to remove me as mayor is unpardonable."

Davies broke in. "I ruined your career. Your marriage? You had an affair with your wife's twin."

"You are vile. My personal life is no business of yours."

"It *is* my business. Your lack of judgment, as mayor, is the people's business. Philander on your own time."

The mayor's face was as red as a rash. Blinded by rage, he couldn't speak. He muttered something into his coat pocket. In an instant, Reg's men entered the room. Anna, who'd been quiet up to this point, got up and pulled a revolver from her purse. Everyone who had been seated stood up in shock. Maggie screamed. It was impossible to breathe.

Liam heard shouting from the other room. He ran in to see what was happening. He found everyone wrapped around the oval conference table in the bizarre form of a firing squad. The henchmen drew their pistols. Three guns were aimed in the direction of George

Davies.

Dan jumped from his chair, pulled a badge from his jacket, and showed his gun. "FBI. Drop your weapons."

Dan was an undercover agent who was only using Davies to track Anna. The FBI now surrounded the building. Anna reasoned she must shoot her way out. Reg's plan was abandoned. She fired the first shot. Davies, grabbing his chest, hit the ground with a dead thump. Reg's men started shooting. Gadly and Caitlin lowered their heads and ran from the room. Dan killed Reg's men with precision and Anna put a bullet in his shoulder — his pitching arm — folding him at the knees. Mayor Binks and Reg sprinted for the door, pushing Liam aside. Then Anna put Maggie in her sights. Maggie knew too much. Anna needed her dead. She fired a shot. Liam jumped in front of Maggie and intercepted the bullet in his neck. Maggie, white as paper, screamed and threw herself on top of him. As Anna made her way to the door, Maggie reached for the assassin's ankle and put her on the ground. Dan's agents entered the building, blocking Reg and Binks from escaping. Dan, wounded but still moving, now had Anna in custody.

Maggie placed her hand — soaked in blood — over the open wound in Liam's neck. As she held him in her arms, she felt life leave his body—he was gone. Maggie secured his head in her chest, rocking it from side to side. She wailed in agony. As the discord of agents and criminals moved around her, she held tight to his lifeless body. She wouldn't dare let go of him.

They had never been closer than the day of his death. Liam's final act saved Maggie's life. She used to tell him how he'd saved her all those years ago when they first fell in love.

Liam spent his life writing fiction not only to explain the human condition but to understand an imperfect world. In his books, he could cure the incurable. But that's not how things are in the real world. With imagination, he wrote above the limitations of possibility. He could not compose narratives outside the pages he controlled. The best he could do was save Maggie's life. He could not save his own.

25

Onward

The mail was on the kitchen table. Some bills and even more junk to be recycled. The envelopes were addressed in Liam's name. The senders didn't know Liam was dead. But the mail kept coming.

Maggie stayed in the apartment, comforted by the idea of Liam's ghost in the rooms. She wouldn't wash his clothes. His scent, a reminder that he was here. Maggie lived with the weight of depression on her heart. Her company name, *L&M*, was a dedication to their life together. Liam had pushed away her insecurities. He'd pushed her out of harm's way, avoiding Anna's bullet. Saving Maggie's life.

The TV show carried on with Jack and Abam. Maggie had possession of Liam's works—an unpublished novel, numerous short stories, a mass of essays, and random writings.

Maggie wanted to leave Nashville but needed to stay. She didn't want to live in a home Liam never knew. It was a permanency she couldn't handle. Not now. She still sobs, but the warmth of their apartment helps with the sadness.

Jack and Abam plan to bring Liam's unpublished novel to Broadway.

Recalling a conversation with Liam explaining why he envisioned his stories on a live stage, Maggie could still hear his voice.

"What is it about the stage?" she asked.

"The immediacy of the performance. Like a great jazz musician improvising, composing in real time. A live actor works in the same way. Yes, the lines and the plot — like a song — are written, but anything can happen. That's what's exciting." Liam animated his arms. He continued. "Stage actors won't perform the same way every night. Each performance is fleeting. Special to *that* audience. What happens in the day affects the behavior at night. Did the actor fight with her partner? Anxiety over world events. Late on rent. These things seep into the portrayal. Audiences don't react the same way. American audiences are different from European ones. Etcetera, etcetera. Broadway attracts the world's crowd. It's exciting, special, it will only happen once. It's where stories jump to life. Where they live. And the audience *is* the experience." Liam wasn't done. "Being on stage is like riding a wave. Part of the exhilaration is knowing you survived."

Maggie had more days like this. She reflected on individual conversations or little memories. Like the time Liam decided he'd take over grocery shopping and spend too much money on a load of ingredients that couldn't be cobbled together into any real dish. It helped her through the pain of losing him—it was difficult to use his name, at times. There is no getting over losing a loved one. Maggie doesn't want to get over it, but she's learning to adapt and carry on without Liam in her life. She still wears the engagement ring. Someday she'll take it off. Not only to shower or before the gym. But one last time. To the box it came in. Then to a drawer. And life will just… go on. That makes her sad. It will get easier. That, too, makes her sad. The pain will fade, so will Liam. Her heart was closed. Someday that will change.

Looking back to that fateful day — Maggie sometimes allowed herself to — she saw that it took a tragedy to remove a curse. Everything in her world went upside down in a single shot. Her colleague, Dan Benchman, was an FBI agent. Michael's jokes, years ago in Chicago, were prescient. The primary target of the operation was Anna. As impressed with himself as he was, George Davies played only a bit part in this tragedy. Davies and his deceased partner, Charlie Cheney, operated — for years — in the foggy zone between legal and illegal. Anna, as she named herself, was the prize. She didn't blur the line of legality; instead, she blew past it as one would speed through a caution signal. The world they shared was deception, fraud, and trickery. But they played small ball while Anna starred in the big leagues. After her arrest, she cut a deal with the government to help bring down her most powerful allies. The money laundering schemes that touched everyone from George Davies to Gus Tower all led to Anna. She cultivated a web of clients around the world who wanted influence in American political affairs. The United States was the ultimate prize. The world's greatest superpower was becoming a whale—weak and in decline. Because of her efforts, shady demagogues now held the keys to power in governments worldwide. Autocrats took their unscrupulous private sector practices and applied them to government, leading to an all-out assault on democratic norms. Where they come from, checks and balances don't exist. Once elected, they dismantled the emergency brakes of democracy and subverted the rule of law for personal gain. The modern autocrat's ideology is raw power, self-dealing. In hindsight, the moves were predictable: attack the press, weaken the courts, rewrite the Constitution, and dissolve the separation of powers to saturate power in one place. America is not immune to this disease.

The voters are uniform, bitter, and easy to manipulate. News outlets don't prioritize information. Or news. The advertising dollars sustaining these organizations relies on outrage. Fear and anger sell subscriptions. The best way for cable news to keep their ratings high is to rocket the blood pressure of the people watching at home. The absurdity feeds itself in a perpetual loop of rage, ignorance, and credulity. What is terrifying is how easy it was to get here.

Returning to Anna, the sham companies she started

created a way to move dirty money and opened a path to fund political campaigns. She was a Czech national living in Switzerland. She met George Davies at a political event in DC. He introduced her to Gus Tower. That's how she came to be in Gadly's world. Gadly wasn't involved with their crimes though he was willfully blind to their operations. Gadly benefited from his proximity to power. He fed his business in a way that kept his hands clean.

Mayor Binks was thirsty for revenge. The ruin of the mayor's distinguished career ended up being the least of his problems. He was now an accessory to the murder of Gus Tower. Reg had a long history of crimes that lost opacity under the light of this affair. Anna hired him when she needed to strong-arm a client though they hadn't murdered anyone prior to hanging Gus Tower. Both Reg and Mayor Binks are put away for a long time. Anna's sentence is still pending as she continues to assist law enforcement.

And that brings us to Caitlin and Gadly—the most complicated part of this story. The mystery of who poisoned Charlie Cheney was never solved—only Caitlin and Gadly know the truth. Agent Benchman has a hunch but instead thinks of Caitlin and Gadly as assets to his successful mission. He didn't do much digging after Charlie turned up poisoned. The FBI was after Anna because, without her, the entire operation would have crumbled.

The special election for mayor happened with the

scandal. Gadly closed his business. He and Caitlin quietly married and now live in Washington DC, where he works as a consultant. Caitlin continues to assist Gadly with his professional life. She has memory-holed the recent events in the same way she dealt with the death of her daughter, Rebecca.

Gadly entered the room and touched her shoulder.

Caitlin smiled but didn't look up.

He said, "Do you suppose we'll stay in Washington? I only ask because you have eyes on France."

"The truth is, I'd like to end up in France. Leaving Nashville felt like a chapter ending. But leaving America would close the book."

Without prodding too much, Gadly understood what she meant. He struggled with his justifications for murdering Charlie. On some days he was confident in his reasons but other times he couldn't ignore the guilt. Occasionally, lying awake at night, he'd tempt himself to go to the police and turn himself in. Gadly would think of calling up Dan Benchman to confess his crime. But he feared a life without Caitlin more than he feared his guilty conscience. Gadly wouldn't dare seek advice from Caitlin on this for the chance it might change her mind about him. She'd endured so much. Gadly didn't want to be the cause of more pain. What made them work well together was that he gave her a place to lay her heart. It was in this place, with Gadly, that Caitlin could send her grief out to sea. Here, she forgave herself for failing Rebecca. Caitlin also created justifications for looking past the poisoning of her husband. Gadly had saved her life. A dreadful deed created the balance necessary for her to survive. In her marriage to Charlie, she felt like a castaway. Then Gadly came along with a rescue boat. He did what he had to do.

Gadly said, "I think we shouldn't wait too long to leave. Let's leave it all, everything, behind us." He sat down. "I survived the death of my wife. I learned to live alone—for a while anyway. I feel like we are always trying to outrun old versions of ourselves. Let's not give them the chance to catch up."

"What will become of your work?" Caitlin said.

"We don't need the money. Aren't you tired of running?"

"Yes. And France sounds like the perfect place to stop."

Gadly paused to think. He rested his chin on his hand. Caitlin walked to him. Sat in his lap. For a silent moment, they stared at each other. Caitlin knew she was staring into the eyes of the man who had murdered her husband. She also knew she was fine with it.

Rita, living in London with Jack and Abam, will be a grandmother. They will call him Amis. Jack quit acting to focus on directing. He also started the Harrison Foundation to support up-and-coming writers and artists. Part of the foundation will fund an arts and literature program at his former high school in Kansas

City—where he met Liam.

Jack found it hard to conceal his despair. He'd noticed someone on the street, thinking it was Liam. Other times, he thought he heard Liam's voice. Jack was depressed and couldn't pull himself up. Everything seemed meaningless.

Abam was patient with him.

"You are dark. Wishing to trade places with Liam. But where would that leave you? He'd be grieving the loss of his best friend just as you are now. You should weep for your friend. We weep for Maggie. Nothing about this is fair or right. But nihilism isn't the answer."

Jack was silent. He felt hollow inside.

Abam continued. "You go on by celebrating his life. You do what you are doing right now with the foundation." She explained the immortality in Liam's work. In that way, he's a lucky one. Most people leave only memories behind. Memories are special, but they fade. Liam left behind words, stories that outlive him. His light will carry on with his works. His beat goes on within Maggie. She said, "And he lives on inside of you."

They wept together.

Maggie cabbed from the hotel in SoHo to Chelsea. Navigating the big city on her own—like her life without Liam. She got out in Chelsea and walked around without an itinerary. Maggie's heels clicked on the streets of the city Liam adored. She used to ask him why he called New York his favorite place on Earth. "Because New York looks and sounds like the world."

The wind scattered the clouds, except for one. Maggie was alone.

She brought Liam's ashes to New York and spread them in Central Park. During the afternoon, she sipped on coffee and spoke to Liam, like an echo of him remained alive, or semi-alive. She giggled at an obscene word scribbled onto a construction zone. Walking by a young couple, Maggie wondered what they were talking about. She imagined conversations she might have with Liam but were no longer possible.

Gravity was rearranged. Maggie didn't feel sorrowful at this moment. She was grateful for the time with Liam — the limits of time and the distance that was also limited but now permanent and in the dark valleys of fading memories she'll hurry for a candle to light for a little more time to laugh or to cry or to curse the god she doesn't believe in, the hard finality of life, the unfairness which is also why it's beautiful which is also why she makes plans and a plan is an intention which is a process for healing wounds and what Maggie needs most now is healing — an inescapable part of her journey.

Under the sun, she stared at her ring. It looked like Champagne. Champagne split apart by green gemstones. Like Maggie and Liam. Split apart. Maggie shining under the sun. Liam returned to the soil. She planned to remove the ring when she got back to

Nashville. Maggie would put the box away. The box would house the ring like a museum holding history to prove it really happened. She was sure she'd open the box, studying the past from time to time when she wanted to laugh and weep over memories. But she'd never wear the ring again.

On her final night in New York, she walked under the vivid lights on the way to watch a rendition of *West Side Story*. By habit, she bought two tickets.

Maggie saw the future recede among the thieves and selfish liars but refused to drown in the currents of cynicism. She escaped the eddy. Maggie could have surrendered to the obscene, but she didn't. She moved onward and the ground beneath her feet steadied. Tomorrow will bring with it a new morning. This morning she woke up feeling ill. It was a sensation in her stomach she hadn't felt before. Maggie was sure it was nothing and carried on with her day.

END

Printed in the USA
CPSIA information can be obtained
at www.ICGtesting.com
JSHW020857011023
49210JS00005B/132